D1490897

Close Enemies

A Story of Betrayal

Nyree Hayes

outskirtspress

DENVER, COLORADO

Close Enemies
A Story of Betrayal
All Rights Reserved.
Copyright © 2012 Nyree Hayes
v2.0

Cover Photo © 2012 mocker / www.fotosearch.com. All rights reserved - used with permission.

Outskirts Press, Inc.
http://www.outskirtspress.com

ISBN: 978-1-4327-9684-6

Outskirts Press and the "OP" logo are trademarks belonging to Outskirts Press, Inc.

PRINTED IN THE UNITED STATES OF AMERICA

Acknowledgements

I would first like to Give All Honor to God, without him none of this would have been possible. I want to Give a very special thanks to my best friend, my fiancé Earnest Brown. He is my motivation and pushes me to achieve my dreams, and stood beside me to help make this happen. I would like to thank my mother, Gladys Guy, for being down and believing in me!

Be Blessed...

Chapter 1
"OG"

I awoke with the uncomfortable feel of sweat from sleeping. I looked at the alarm clock on the nightstand. 2:57 am. The two-bedroom apartment was as silent as a church at this time of night as I sat on the side of the bed holding my head in my hands. It was definitely too quiet. But quietness is what I love right now. Being that I just did a four-year bid. And within those four years I had never been alone. There was always someone around.

When I awoke, when I laid to sleep, when I took a shit, ate, showered, everything. Now here I was on my second day out and the quietness is now uncomfortable. I went into the bathroom to let out my morning issue of urine and gas. It felt weird to be alone but good at the same time. I looked in the mirror at my handsome chiseled face and smiled, happy to be out of that hellhole. The last four years were the worst years of my life and I refuse to relive it.

I went into the living room of the plush apartment. My baby's momma, Tiffany, found the five hundred a month apartment with a balcony and hooked it up. I sat in front of the computer and turn it on. It was the first thing I told her to buy. I had earned an Associate's Degree in my last two years in prison to avoid the crowd that I had been hanging with. I was trying to think of something better than selling Dope.

And the Dope game was good right now. My best friend Javon, known to everybody as "Oil Can" was in it to win. Oil Can had connected with some weight in Texas. So he was knee deep in the streets of Pine Bluff, Arkansas. I went to Microsoft Word and typed the big homies a letter:

What up,

It feels good ya'll. This my second night and I can't sleep. I haven't even fucked anything yet! I got my mind on this money. I told G-man before I left that I was through with the streets and was going to invest money in some type of business. I'm going to send ya'll some money off with this. Ya'll nigga's be good.

Yo nigga,

OG

I hit print and made an envelope up. It was now 4:15 am on a Tuesday morning. I was restless but didn't know where I wanted to start my life. As I set there staring at the monitor I thought about Tiffany and my four-year-old daughter Malicia. Tiffany was pregnant when I got locked down and I watched my daughter grow from visits. Tiff and I had been on bad terms when I left for my bid. We came to an understanding for Malicia. I love my daughter to death and I'm going to spoil her ass. And everybody knows it. Tiff and I both be fronting like we're so over with each other. But we both are crazy about each other. And everybody else knows it. I miss having sweaty sex and the feel of her beautiful five foot eight frame. Tiff was a yellow bone with big black round eyes with jet-black baby hair going down the small of her back. A nice set of c-cups, a six-pack, with the precise amount of ass and hips made her physic.

At twenty-six years of age, she was a Nurse and a student that loved thug niggas. I looked at a picture of our daughter on the computer table. I could see her in Malicia's features. Those big pretty eyes that seemed to glow, the same beautiful skin as her mother. We had made an angel. My baby was smart too.

"Daddy why come you're not living with momma and me?" She had asked on our last visit behind bars. "Cause baby, your mom needs her space right now." I lied.

Tiffany had a boyfriend and I was a single man capable of fucking a whole lot of women. And Tiffany hated that fact. I been seeing it in her body language that she wanted to be the first to get the stick, but her nigga might get in the way. She was fucking with some guy out of a hood called The Mob and he knew who I was. I was deep in the streets before I left and can jump back knee deep with my street cred. They not only call me OG because of my government, Octavious Green, but I was OG status and had just done four years for the hood.

I went back into the bedroom and dialed up Oil on my new cell phone. A Young Jeezy ring tone was loud enough to hear across the room.

"Who this?" my best friend answered in the same gritty voice as usual.

"Its me."

"Oh snap! What up my nigga! Where are you at?" Oil Can asked excited to hear my voice.

"I'm at the crib. Where you at?"

"On my way back from Memphis. Nigga I'm coming to get you today, I don't give a fuck about all that being alone shit, and nigga we going shopping! Nigga the hood wants to see you nigga!" Oil Can said in a high pitch. "I'm spending today with ME-ME and Tiff and then you know momma wants her time!" I said walking around the apartment admiring the newness.

"Whatever nigga. You and me are tighter than any of the people you just named, but you got till Friday nigga. And get some pussy nigga, besides your baby momma!" Oil can teased.

By 6am I was sitting on the extremely soft sofa drinking coffee and watching CNN. I had picked the coffee habit up in prison. The last four years did not fly by. It went at the pace of time when you want it to move. With the momentum of a snail yet I endured, and here I was, back free. I didn't want to live at a hundred miles per hour no more. Prison opened my eyes to see beyond the hood. Being one of the founders of my hood entitles me to jump back in it full fledge.

And I could have my cake and eat it too. But years of separation from the hood, along with the growing love for my daughter has changed that. I've been blessed to be able to have her love from day one. Thanks to Tiffany and momma who had her there to see me every week. I looked at the TV Screen at the troops in Iraq surrounding a van that had exploded earlier that day. I had also came to find that the rest of the world outside the hood was crazy. There was a lot going on from religion to war. Prison makes you look at everything.

I was twenty-seven years old now and had lost everything when I left. It was the beginning of the year 2007 and by this summer I plan to have my own business. I looked at the cover of the Driver's License book I had been studying for the last two months and found Tiffany's cell number. I had everybody's number on it. A Keysha Cole ring tone played a couple seconds.

"Is you alright?" Tiffany asked concerned.

"Yeah I'm straight, how you know it was me?"

"I bought the phone boy, remember?" Tiffany chuckled and exhaled. "Why you calling me so early, don't you got a booty call with you?"

"Yep. It was good too!" I lied to see if I could detect a hint of jealousy.

"Good. Maybe Me-Me will have your undivided attention today," Tiffany speaking of our daughter to hide the jealousy. "Where yo man at?"

"Where do you think? Right here with his woman! Baby, get up, OG says hi." Tiffany said and I could hear him mumble something.

"What time you coming to get me?" I asked looking at Barack Obama on the screen. "When I get up." I asked in an unimpressed tone.

"Octavious. Don't start with me. Be ready when I get there, understand?" Tiffany said with that lawyer-stating-facts type of voice she uses. "Girl stop! Have yo ass here at eight. Bye." I said and hung up. Cursing me out on the phone was not enough for her, she would wait till she got here. An hour later after barely dozing off she was knocking on the door.

"Daddy!" Malicia ran into my arms when I opened the door. I picked her up and rubbed noses and gave her a big wet kiss as she giggled. "Stop Daddy!"

Tiffany was looking up side my head. I could tell she couldn't wait to say her peace. Those big pretty eyes said it all. She was looking like candy as usual. I had been working out the last four years and was chiseled at six foot seven.

"Hey baby, how daddy's angel doing?" I asked Malicia as Tiffany walked past bumping into me with attitude. I shut the door as Tiffany calmly walked around the apartment as if I didn't know she was looking for my booty call. She got in my face as I held our daughter in my arms. "Let me tell you something. First, don't ever hang up in my face." Tiffany said with her finger pushing my head. Malicia looked back and forth at us giggling.

"Second, you are on my time!" She finished, picking a piece of lint out of Malicia's hair. I stared at Tiffany's lips that were shining with lip-gloss. I gave her a look that said I wanted to suck them. Both pair.

"N-E-way!" She responded to my look and smacked her exposed set.

"Daddy, mommy says I have my own room here too!" Malicia said kicking her legs.

"Yes you do, let mommy show you while I take a shower and get ready." I said and she eased down. "I just need a few minutes!" I was responding to Tiffany's look of not believing I wasn't ready.

I came out the shower with a towel wrapped around my waist. I wanted to see Tiff's face when she saw my new solid muscles over my dark frame. She was on the computer with her back to me on the phone. I walked up and tapped her on the shoulder. She turned in the chair and looked up at me with her mouth hanging open. She forgot her conversation and roamed my body from chest to dick print.

"What are you looking at?" I asked pleased with her response.

"N-E-way! I got a man!" She rolled her eyes, cleared her throat and turned back around. "N-E-way girl, what were you saying?"

"Hey," I said in her ear, "I lied. I *still* haven't been with no one. And when it's said and done," I turned her face to face mine, "I'm still in love with you and is going to get you and my daughter back."

"Think so?"

"Know so." I said and stepped back and dropped my towel. Tiffany eyes got big with lust and got a good look at my dick before looking in my face.

"Boy! ME-ME is in the next room, cover yo ass up before she sees your crazy tail!" She demanded moving back down to my package. She started fidgeting with the computer, which meant she was turned on. I put the towel back on. I had won this round.

Chapter 2
"OIL CAN"

Iam so glad that my guy is out. In the last four years I have not found anyone that could replace my best friend since seventh grade. Half of this shit out here is his. The click is getting money and we can fuck any broad out here. A lot of things done changed since my guy left.

"Oil Can! Nigga are you gone pass the blunt or what nigga!" A member of the click named Pimp asked.

"Nigga don't you see me in my mothafuckin thoughts nigga?" I said with the screwface. I had forgot I was chilling in one of our dope houses smoking weed and getting this money. I passed the blunt.

"What's up with that nigga OG? That nigga still on that positive shit?" Pimp asked between hits of the blunt.

"Hell yeah, nigga just talking right now. Nigga don't know how it is yet. Don't see all this money we getting right now." I said accepting the blunt back. Pimp released his smoke.

"What time is the surprise party?"

"Be there at eleven sharp. The nigga don't know yet but I'll get him there. And hey, get them twins for me." I said and passed the blunt as another Trapstah named Cool came from the back with a few niggas that was copping some ounces of some good green. After letting the dudes out, he stood in front of Pimp and me with his pants sagging a little too hard. His Trapstah Gangsta piece and chain hanging to his stomach.

"When I'mma see my nigga OG? Why that nigga hiding and shit?" Cool said sitting his 40 Cal on the coffee table then pulling his pants up and buckling his belt buckle full of diamonds.

"Friday you know that nigga's baby momma got him on lock right now." I said counting my money for the hundredth time. I don't know why but every nigga I know does this ritual.

"That girl doesn't play neither, with her mean ass!" Pimp said handing Cool the blunt. My ring tone kicked in.

"What up?"

"Hey, is this Oil Can?" A feminine voice asked.

"Yeah. Who this?" I asked confused cause I had a gang of females wanting to be on the team. "This is Lamira, from Fayetteville. We met in the club Motions' the other night?"

"Ah shit, what up girl! I was waiting on you to call shawty!" I lied. I didn't know whom I was talking to.

"Fa real?" Lamira asked.

"Fa real. I'm diggin you shawty. What you living like right now? I mean, are you free this week?" I asked.

"Yeah! I'll be free Friday after work, and I got to go get my car out the shop. Why come you didn't call me like you said you was? I'm hoping you were busy. "Lamira said with the sweetest voice.

"I stay busy shawty. But I'mma make time to get with your fine ass!" I said and she giggled. I didn't know what she looked like but when I hung up I would be looking through the phone for a picture.

"Don't forget me!" she sung.

"I won't. You be good shawty I got work to do." I said and hung up. I scrolled through my phone till I found her. A chocolate almond eyed delight with a bright smile.

"Look at this hoe my nigga. Bitch *bad* isn't she?" I said and passed the phone to Cool who paused *Madden 07* him and Pimp was playing.

"Damn!" Cool said.

"Let me see nigga?" Pimp said and looked at the snap shot. "Same night?"

"Bet." I said agreeing to a bet that I would hit the same night. "My charger against yo Magnum?"

"Bet nigga." Pimp said and we did our handshake. I put Jeezy's "I Got Money" on the CD boom box and started counting my money again. My thoughts went back to OG. I missed my nigga and needed him by my side. There aren't too many nigga's out here built like him. Snitching is an underrated epidemic out here.

"I hope them nigga's from ole boy click don't go fucking with OG for murkin that nigga." Cool said referring to the Eastside Pirus. OG had killed one of their leaders. "Man fuck them niggas! They aren't gone fuck with my nigga!" Pimp said and pulled the AK 47 from under the sofa. Pimp had one of the ugliest screwfaces that scared the average person. A new blunt dangled from his lips as he spoke. "Little niggas better get that little paper they getting and stay the fuck back! Make me show them how Trapstah niggas make it do what it do!"

"No mothafuckin doubt!" I said as Cool cell phone vibrated on the table.

"Where yall at? Aight, bet." Cool said then hung up. "Nigga that's them hoes wanting them X pills. They outside." He opend the door after Pimp put the AK back up. I watched through the blinds as a redbone and a white girl strolled up. They came in and Cool went back through the procedure of locking the four locks on the door.

"Man, that smells good!" Red bone spoke referring to the weed. She was real cute in her Prada outfit and pink Air Force Ones. "Yall niggas got some of that for sale?"

"Yep. What yall want?" Cool asked since he was the one that knew them.

"Girl we need an ounce of that shit!" The white girl said to red-bone. She had on a Baby Phat blue jean suit with ass and hips. Both of their faces were pretty.

"This shit four hundred an ounce shawty." Cool said as I went back off in my thoughts. I already had more broads than I needed.

I left the trap in my new 2010 Corvette that I was really feeling right now. All the hoes say I look like a little boy sitting down low in it. Most people say I look like T.I since we got the same skin tone and size.

I made a left down Cherry Street heading home. I felt my main cell vibrating my hip. I already knew who it was.

"Where the fuck is you at?" Honey yelled in my ear. Honey was my main bitch. A Hershey Chocolate standing at five foot five with much attitude. And some mean dick-sucking skills.

"Man, I'm chasing paper. What's up?" I said hiding my other cell in a stash spot under the dash. "You bet not be calling me about some bullshit!:"

"Man, what time you coming home, this shit is getting cold and I'm about to lay down cause my head is hurting. Will you please come home?" Honey asked. I can see her fine ass now. I met her a year ago and decided to keep her for a while. Just like the rest of them she was trying to tie me down. I had an incoming call.

"Hold on?" I clicked over. "What it is?"

"Say nigga, this that nigga Shine, what the weather like?" Shine asked in code for some work. "Good nigga, I got the top down," I said asking what he wanted.

"Come scoop a nigga I got two bad bitches with some double D's. "He said wanting nine ounces.

"Bet. Meet me at Mommas." I said giving him a spot to meet and then clicking over. "Baby I'm back."

"Baby I need some dick right now to take this headache away. Come give me some of that big ole dick!" Honey moaned seductively and it made my dick jump.

"Guess what? I'm in the driveway." I hung up and pulled up behind my Cutlass and beside her Chevy Tahoe. I walked in the house and before I could shut the door good and lock it, Honey had me up against it. She had on a tank top and panties.

"Hey baby! I miss you so much!" Honey said and sucked my bottom lip while unbuckling my pants. She dropped down and pulled my dick out through the hole in my boxers then gently stroked and kissed it. "You missed me baby?" She asked between licks and kisses looking up at me. I was rock hard.

"No doubt. I missed yo ass girl!" I said and she went to sucking with no hands, and then ran them up my flat stomach while slurping and moaning.

"Ooh, yo dick taste so good!"

"Do that shit baby." I said barely holding back. She went to deep throating and massaging my balls. I exploded and she kept going and swallowed everything. She put my man back up just as clean as it was from when she pulled it out.

Chapter 3
"Lamira"

I can't believe that nigga had fell for that stunt I pulled on his ass. I mean, the way them niggas be talking about how he's a killer and this and that, I should be able to get next to this nigga in no time. I thought he was T.I when I first seen him.

"May I please use your phone to see if my daughter is okay? I can't get a signal." I had asked him that night in the club. Him and some more guys from his crew were shining, taking pictures with a gang of females while I stood on the sideline till I felt my timing was right. He looked at me with fierce eyes and gradually gave me his phone.

"Hurry up." He had said and placed his hands back on the girl he was taking a picture with. I could tell he was popping ecstasy cause he was grinding his teeth. I acted as if I *had* a daughter and turned my back. When he switched females for the pictures I quickly added my number and picture to a long list already entered. I had barely finished when someone spun me around.

"The fuck you doing?" He asked with a twisted screwed face and blood shot eyes. "Nobody's answering, I gotta go." I said and left the club.

"Lamira!" My friend Jaden said with a slap on the arm that brought me out of my thoughts. "You ain't heard shit I said!"

"Girl I heard your ass!" I said. We were leaving McCain Mall with nearly five thousands dollars worth of shit we just boosted. Three down, two more malls to go.

"Mind probably on some nigga." Jaden said and exhaled. I looked at her fat pussy print pushing against her jeans and thought about the time we had got down sexually. We both liked dick and pussy, which probably was why we made good friends.

Of course I disliked some of her ways but when your friends with someone you got to accept the shit you hate along with the good.

"Just thinking about this T.I looking nigga that these Piru niggas got me fucking with. They trying to get to some nigga named OG, but the other nigga name is Oil Can."

"What type of name is that?" Jaden asked.

"Girl I don't know. I've heard one nigga call himself Dick Snot!" I said and we both laughed. "N-E-way, I got to find out them niggas connect, if I do, they gone break me off big time!"

"No, they gone break *us* off." Jaden said matter of fact. "What if Oil Can and OG are boys, since they using Oil to get to OG?"

"Damn girl, your right! I never saw that." I said with thought.

"Then handle Oil, and I'll handle this nigga OG." Jaden said and reached over and rubbed my pussy and gently nibbled my ear. "That's why were the perfect team. We both know how to play our positions!"

"Girl quit before you have a bitch hot and bothered!" I said but it was too late. My pussy was leaking. Certain fabrics can cause me to overheat. Jaden laid back in her seat and started looking through some CD's.

"So after we hit these last two mall's then what?" Jaden asked changing the Trey Songz CD that we were not listening to. "We might as well fuck with our niggas in Hot Springs since I got to go and do my cousin hair. You remember Taneka don't you?"

"Yes, I remember her fine ass!" Jaden said lusting off her thoughts.

"Bitch N-E-way, that's what's up. And tomorrow well formulate a plan for this nigga Oil Can and his boy OG." I said as Lil Boosie came over the system.

"Already." Jaden said firing up a blunt. "All fuckin ready."

Chapter 4
"Tiffany"

I have been sitting her for the last thirty minutes and haven't heard a thing my teacher has said. Every time I try to focus, my mind goes right back to Octavious. And it has been like this for the last three days I've been helping him get situated. I caught myself thinking of the past times we had. From the first time we met to the day we separated on bad terms. The way his click took care of Malicia and me while he was away until I met Neko and literally begged them to stop.

Except for Oil Can, which was like a brother to OG. When OG couldn't reach me and got worried about his daughter, Oil Can was coming. And would find me. I remember the time I was shopping with my man and Oil Can pops up out of nowhere.

"Here." Oil Can had said handing me his cell phone. I was in the middle of finding Malicia an Easter dress. Neko looked At Oil Can like he was crazy but had let it go.

"Hey, I had a dream about ME-ME, ya'll aight?" OG had said. I was so mad I hung up on his ass and cussed him out when I took his daughter to see him the following week. Now he was out and had me going crazy with mixed emotions. Especially after that episode with the dropping of his towel, his chocolate ass was *too* fine! All those muscles with them sexy bow legs. But the shocker was his

Hershey Bar! It was already long but it had gotten thicker. I immediately wanted to run to it and savor the taste of it.

I went home that night and fucked the hell out of Neko. And to tell the truth I wanted to be the first to get the dick but I got a man and my conscience would eat me up if I cheated on him. Neko's a good man. Okay he's a thug, but that's my fetish. Squares just don't do anything for me. Another truth is that, I hope that OG doesn't go back to the streets and sticks to his plan.

It's really hard to tell right now, hell, he won't leave his apartment unless it's with his momma or me. Most times he's on his computer. I wonder if he's gotten him some yet?

I left class and headed to his apartment. OG and ME-ME had been together the last three days, with me taking them here and there. Already he has spent three thousand dollars on clothes and toys, which will stay at his place being that she already had enough stuff at my place. I called Neko.

"Hey baby, what you doing?" I asked all sweet and girly.

"Not shit. Grindin. Aren't you in class?" Neko asked and yawned.

"Nah. I'm through for today. One more year and it's finally over. Your baby will be a Pharmacist. I'm headed over to OG's to get ME-ME. What you want to eat tonight?"

"You!" Neko said. I blushed thinking about his oral skills.

"That's your desert boo!" I said stopping at the light.

"Well, I want my cake and eat it too! Hold on." Neko said and went to doing something. I heard some dudes and the sounds of some locks. "Aight I'm back. You know I'mma tear that ass up tonight, do that Bath and Body scent I like the most. I gotta go, hit me back in a few."

"Aight. I love you baby!" I sung. He repeated my words and hung up.

"Hey baby!' I greeted Malicia after she opened the door. OG was stretched out on the couch with the T.V. on Nickelodeon. "Hey knucklehead." I said pushing OG's arm and sitting on the edge of the couch right in front of that chocolate bar. I did it more out of habit. I would wake him up some nights when we were together and he would listen to what was bothering me and would comfort me.

"How was class?" He said twisting to lie on his back instead of his side. He was shirtless and his six-pack resembled knots under his skin.

"Frustrating as usual. I'll be glad when spring break gets here. What did you all do today?" I asked trying my hardest not to lust. ME-ME helped by walking over and standing between my legs. He went talking about Malicia, how much she sometimes acts just like me. It reminded me how good of a friend Octavious could be. We would sit and talk and be best friends, regardless of the relationship, As if we were meant to be friends, but escalated to a love affair. I was comfortable around him.

"And hey, she even makes that noise you make." OG said with his pretty smile. I made this funny sound with my throat out of habit.

My mother makes the same noise. I used to be embarrassed about it but OG changed that. "No baby, it's not irritating." He had said one day. "It's you. It's a part of you that's unique. It's not loud so you got to know you two know you're doing it. I *love* hearing it. Lets me know I still have you!" He smiled that smile. And I fuck his ass to death! I looked down at my baby. "You over here mocking me girl?" I smiled at ME-ME. She giggled and grabbed my face, pulling for a kiss. I loved the way her strawberry shampoo smelled. She had her daddy's strong chin and pouty lips.

"You said we one mommy! And *you* say I act like daddy!" Malicia said then climb on OG's stomach and I watched them play. I couldn't help but join in and the next thing you know we were all on the floor playing. I had ME-Me by the arms and OG was sitting on her legs with her stretched out on her back.

"Guess what time it is?" OG said and looked at me and I knew what we were about to do.

"It's Tickle Time!" I said. OG and Oil Can had done me like this many of nights because they would come over high as hell with nothing to do.

OG started tickling ME-ME and her crazy tail couldn't get enough and that made us laugh. Then it suddenly got quiet with ME-Me catching her breath and me and OG looking at each other. "Daddy, kiss mommy!" Malicia giggled out.

"What?" I said out of nervousness. Cause Lord knows what might go on if Octavious blessed me with one of his beautiful kisses. He quickly pecked me half on the lips, half on my face. And I realized why he had done it like that. He new I was weak but respected my feelings. He knew that I would leave any man for him. But I would have to make that decision. I also know his ass is about to stay single and fuck damn near ever woman walking cause he knows how I feel about another woman trying to help me raise my daughter.

"Thanks!" I mouthed. He said '*anytime*' with his smile.

Chapter 5
"OG"

It was Friday. Time to face the hood and I was ready to see the world. Oil was at my apartment at five in the morning and we were on the highway fifteen minutes later. I knew my position in the streets and was going to take advantage of that to get out of them. Oil Can had picked me up in the same Vette he had sent a picture of. In the picture he had his chain hanging out the window with diamonds everywhere. But seeing it in person made a lot of difference. He caught me staring at it and smiled displaying a ten thousand dollar platinum and diamond grill.

We couldn't wait to hook up and do the damn thing. Oil and me go way back. Like a Pimp C and Bun B type of way back, and me and his momma are the only people that call him just "Oil". We were doing a good 120 miles per hour. And the Vette handled perfectly.

"Nigga I got a surprise fo yo ass!" Oil said looking young as hell, laid back pushing the whip with ease. "Wait to you see my apartment in the Rock." The Rock was short for Little Rock, Arkansas. "What's up with the business shit?" He asked slowing down for traffic.

"Member I said I wanted to fuck with some barber shops?" I said looking out at the different new vehicles wandering what kind I would be getting.

"Yeah, what it is?"

"Well I thought of some mo shit. Tiff and me was going down Hardin Street and I seen a building for lease. It's a detail shop and a tire place. I'mma make it into a detail shop and a gift shop. Niggas want to shop while their shit getting clean. Nigga we sell clothes, hats and shit. Nigga I been on the Internet networking my nigga. Trust your boy." I looked at my best friend and knew I didn't have to ask but did out of respect. "I need about a hundred though. Can I borrow that and hit you back later on?"

"Nigga already! You didn't even have to ask me no shit like that, ole country ass nigga!" Oil said trying to punch me but I blocked and was about to strike back but thought about how fast we were going.

"Real talk though, we bout to get some real paper my nigga. I can't explain all I got planned. Rome wasn't built over night. With that said, we gone be able to get out the streets my nigga." I said and we did our shake. Along with Oil Can and me, four guys run Trapstah Gangstas click, a click of eighty-seven young infamous thugs. Two of us were incarcerated. We made it to the rock and stopped by Kentucky Fried Chicken.

The world was alive out here. Every woman was looking good. After parking, Oil Can went to a stash spot and got a P90 Gloc. KFC had nothing but women working in it and the girl working our register was cute but had acne across her forehead. We ordered and since no one was behind us, we went back to talking. Oil Can had diamonds everywhere with fresh Air Force Ones, a pair of Evisu Jeans and a White Tee. I had no diamonds with Jeans and Tee. The register girl gave off a look as if wandering if we were together.

"Nigga we going shopping in Dallas. "Oil Can said.

"Texas?"

"Duh nigga!" Oil gave me a light screwface. The food came and we were on our way to his apartment. The complex was gated with security and we pulled beside a black "06" Cadillac STS. I got out looking at the beauty with no tints and Peanut Butter leather throughout it that looked soft. The paint was wet looking as if it should be dripping on the sidewalk, and was equipped with the wood grain steering wheel. We went inside the plush apartment and sat on the leather couch, I turned on the flat screen to CNN as Oil Can twisted on a blunt.

"Nigga put it on videos, fuck the news!"

"Hold on nigga, that's why yo ass don't know shit now. Stuck in fantasyland. "I said holding on to the remote.

"Nigga I don't want to here that ole penitentiary shit! They done fucked yo mind up! You smart my nigga, but don't be acting like shit wrong when you aren't try to do it no mo. Feel dat nigga?" Oil Can said and put fire to the blunt.

"My nigga, I love these streets. I raised the click and niggas respect OG!" I said waiting to hit the blunt. "And if a nigga in my way then I'm murkin something. Feel dat? But I'mma do it smarter and get away ever trip. Prison made me more ruthless my nigga. With some intelligence my nigga, I've had too much time to think."

"My nigga!" Oil Can felt and gave me a hug. I took a hit of the blunt and we were quiet for a minute. We both had a lot on our minds. We finished smoking the blunt and I was high being it was my first time smoking in about two months. Oil Can would give women weed that worked at Varner Unit when I would send them at him. He probably fucked a few of them, in which I wanted him to do, so they would become reliable.

"Here." Oil Can tossed me a key with an alarm pad. It had a Cadillac emblem made into it. "I hope you like it Trapstah!" We did our handshake. My mind shot to the Black beauty I seen outside. I looked at Oil with curiosity then shot to the parking lot and hit the alarm, sure enough she winked at me.

We made it back from Dallas way past nine that night with me driving up there while Oil Can slept, then me sleeping while he drove back. After we unloaded the thirty thousand dollar wardrobe into my living room, we got ready for a party some females were throwing. I got fresh in a green Coogi outfit with some Bape tennis shoes. I had two pinky rings on, full of diamonds, diamond studs in both ear, a matching watch and bracelet, and a diamond cross on a platinum chain hanging to the middle of my chest.

Now I was looking like me and Oil was together. The waves in my hair were in beehive form and prison fresh.

Oil got just as fresh in a Polo fit and boots with his usual diamonds. I remember back when we was barely hustling. He would still wear hands full of rings and chains like we were making lots of money. We both love to dress and use to spend everything but recop money on clothes. We jumped back in my new STS, in which I was in love with at first sight, it rode so smooth with that new smell. I thought about throwing some black rims on it. Maybe some twenties. We made it to some new building in the Bluff and parked, then decided to smoke a blunt on the lot.

"Damn. Everybody sitting on something tall!" I said referring to the rims. I could hear the thump of the beat coming from inside the building.

"Nigga I got a Cutlass on twenty-fours. That bitch goes hard!" Oil Can said coughing and passing the blunt back. "Pop the trunk nigga." He headed to the trunk as I popped it. He called me back and showed me how to pop the stash spot with the alarm remote. The tail light panel eased open revealing two Glocs. He had showed me one under the dash earlier.

We started towards the club. A car was rolling up and we both automatically placed our hands on our pistols. I hadn't toted one in four years but some old habits were hard to break.

The Honda that rolled up with the Delta Sorority tags on it contained four pieces of eye candy. We all exchanged glances as they rolled by and we continued on into the party. After stepping in and seeing most of the dudes I realized that this wasn't a party thrown by some females. My click was throwing this party cause they were the only males in here.

"What up Trapstah?" a youngster by the name of Cool asked with a diamond smile and a hug. I had raised him in the streets. Another youngster named Pimp was at his side.

I had raised him too.

"Hiding and shit!" Pimp said with a bigger smile. "You can't run nigga! You're a Trapstrah at heart nigga!"

"Already!" I smiled and we did our handshake.

"That nigga Oil Can said that you haven't fucked nothing yet! Nigga you gone fuck tonight!" Cool said eyeing all the broads that was here for the click. It seemed as if every girl in here could have been a model. Hurricane Chris' "Ay Bay Bay" was pumping through out the building. It had a swimming pool on the inside and that's where the party was at as we made our way through. I took my time being welcomed back by my click members.

The girls wondered about me but that soon changed once Oil Can made it to the DJ booth. "Listen up mothafuckas! My mothafuckin brotha just got back and is in the mothafuckin building! OG! I love you nigga! Nigga look what we created!" Oil Can said with a champagne bottle held in the air. I was making my way to him giving handshakes to click members as I did. "Get up here nigga!" Oil Can demanded. I made it to him and grabbed the mic.

"What up everybody?" I said feeling odd for some reason. "I got a confession to make. "The crowd made an 'ooh!' sound that floated across the room. "I've changed alot. I just did four years for the hood and had a whole lot of time to think. I talked a lot to the big homies and I have their blessings to make it do what it do. We bout to get this paper, real talk, as a matter of fact, we gone turn this here party into a business venture. I'll get back to that in a minute. Right now I'm about to come down there to all these honies cause I haven't been intimate in the last four days that I have been free!" I said as the ladies screamed and yelled out different promises.

"Let me handle that! "…

"I got you over here baby!"…

"Come to me with yo chocolate self!

I whispered in the DJ ear and The Dream's "Shawty da Shit" came to life. I came down from the booth and my click surrounded me giving the females no room to get their Mack on. We moved to the pool area where two-piece swimsuits were displaying flesh that was looking tastey. Two girls had tag teamed a Trapstah and threw him in the pool. Two females were kissing on one end of the pool while other Trapstahs mingled with the other girls and got blunted on the other side.

"Oh snap!" Nigga that's the bitch I called on our way back!" Oil Can said tapping my arm. A habit he's had forever. I followed his eyes and seen a Black Stallion and a Yellow Clydesdale coming in our direction. Clydesdale was bowlegged with straps from her Stilettos up to her knees complementing her wrap around skirt. She was a few inches shorter than me and I wanted to taste those long legs. Black Stallion wasn't bad looking neither.

"Hey Oil Can!" The Stallion said to Oil giving him a hug. Her booty was perfect in her Apple Bottoms.

"What it is girl?" Oil Can said and then tapped her arm.

"Ay, this my nigga OG," He looked at me, "This here Lamira. Who's your friend?"

"This is my B.F.F Jaden." Lamira said. Her skin was smooth and fresh looking.

"Hey how yall doing?" That was Jaden. Her skin was also flawless.

"I'm good." I said looking at Jaden. "And I've just found who I wanted to bring my summer in with. Fine as you is, your mind has got to be just as beautiful!" I finished as she tried to conceal a blush.

"Thank you! That was real sweet! You trying to get chose aren't you playa?" Jaden said displaying a set of braces and dimples.

"Already!" I said giving a sexy screwface, and one on those loo-kovers from head to toe that would make my baby momma Tiffany feel naked.

And now it had the same affect on this yellow sculpture of beauty.

"Boy, you are a hot mess!" Jaden smiled and cocked her head to the side. "Would you like a drink?"

"That's what's up!" I said and grabbed her from behind and started our way to the bar.

"I know I'm half ass wrong for invading your space like this but I couldn't stop the wanting to be near you!" I said in her ear as we slowly walked. Her hands were at her side with mine intertwined. One of her soft ass cheeks bumped into my pelvis.

"I can not believe I'm hearing this!" She smiled out. "You say shit that sound so lame but yet so sweet! She looked up at me. Cool passed by and we nodded at each other.

"Girl, it's up to me at this present moment that I could decide to rather make you fall in love and be the one, or call it quits in the morning." I said.

"Nigga it was on me that you've made it this far!" Jaden said with fresh breath. We made it to the bar. She ordered four shots of Pa'tron as we sat and got good looks at each other. "Where did you accomplish all that confidence?" Jaden asked after throwing back a shot of Patron.

"It wasn't confidence!" I said and did the same.

"Then what was it?"

"You wanted this!" I eyed her.

"How you figure?"

"You're body was calling me when you entered the room!" I said and downed my second shot. She blushed. "Bartender… yeah, let me get an Apple Martini, Pina Colada, four more shots of Pa'tron and whatever you drinking." I turned back to Jaden. "What's your favorite drink?"

"Ooh Apple Martini!" Jaden said looking sexy by the eyes and lips.

"You seem to fit a Martini, real smooth and very easy going down!"

"What?" She smiled all cute with her little sexy mean mug.

"Girl, I'm just bullshittin. N-E way, what's up? Let's get away and just kick it, turn this into a date. Meet me here in an hour. I'mma make a few announcements, fuck with my niggas, look at a few more women, check out your competition!" I said and placed some of her loose hair back behind her ear. I gently rubbed down the side her face with the back of my hand. "You fuckin with a Gangsta tonight!" I said and pulled out my phone and handed it to her. She put her number in and I got a snap shot of her pretty face. "In case I decide to leave early." I said and down another shot, really feeling the alcohol. She took out her phone and did the same routine. "In case I decided I didn't go!" Jaden said looking at her Martini, then took a sip while giving me a sideward glance.

"That's what's up!" I said and strolled off with my drink, two stepping my way through the crowd. It felt good to be free.

Chapter 6

"Jaden"

I watched his sexy ass stroll off and sipped my Martini. This nigga had game, *and* he was fine! I wanted to leave immediately and fuck his brains out. But I had to remember that I was helping my girl out and was on a job. I knew plenty of fine niggas with some good dick, but I wanted to try his ass out. I was brought out of my thoughts when one of these Trapstah niggas approached me. He had diamonds everywhere, but his game was nowhere to be found. He was way younger than twenty-three. I politely declined his offer of being his freak for the night. I heard OG get on the mic with Oil Can by his side. The DJ put on Young Jeezy's *"Trap or Die"* and every nigga in here song it word for word in unison as if it was their theme song. I went to find Lamira. I found her by the pool.

"Girl, this party is off the chain! I see about ten nigga's I could fuck!" Lamira said. I could tell she was tipsy by the way she kept licking her lips. "I see a few hoes I could do too!" "About fifteen! Look at that redbone, white Stilettos. Think she'll go?" I asked really feeling the girls presence. My cell vibrated. I read the text: you ready? **OG.** I text him back: No. **J.** I looked up to a Trapstah in Lamira's face trying to get his Mack on.

"Excuse me playa, I need to holla at my woman for a second." I said and pulled her by the hands to the side. "This nigga OG just text me. I'm about to bounce with him and do what it do." I said. The liquor had me feeling good. Something caused me to look up and OG was making his way to me. "Girl, here he comes. Call me in an hour." I said as he made it to me.

"Come on." OG said and grabbed my hand. I abided as he led the way.

I turned and waved bye to Lamira.

We hopped in his car with the new smell, snuggled in, and made conversation as we hit the highway.

"Why you go to prison?" I asked taking my heels off.

"Manslaughter charge. Some shit with the click." OG said looking sexy behind the wheel.

"You look like you fresh out too!" I said watching him.

"Why is that?"

"Cause, you know, the waves, the clear skin, the body. You are too fine to have been running the streets." I said grabbing one of his big arms.

"You trying to make a nigga blush aren't you?" He said displaying a nice smile.

"Nigga please! You probably hear that shit all the time. I know you might already got a gang of hoes jocking!" I said watching his eyes. "And why is you lying like you haven't fuck nothing yet?" I said placing my hands between my thighs, Listening.

"I been with my daughter all week. She was born while I was locked up. She's four and that's the only woman I've been interested in. I could've fucked baby momma but that will complicate things." OG said and I all of a sudden felt that I could trust him. "You got any kids?" "Nope" I lied. My baby girl Asia will be two in a few weeks. He put in a Pretty Ricky CD and let it softly tickled our ears. We were quiet for a while. I slightly bobbed my head to the music. I caught him watching me.

"Boo nigga!" I said and rolled my eyes. He reached over and

placed some hair behind my ear. "Can I keep you?" OG asked.

"What?"

"I mean, if we fuck or not tonight, I like your style. I see a lot of potential in you. You special. I'm tipsy right now but I'm telling you some real shit girl." He grabbed my hand and kissed it. "I'm the truth, all you got to do is be the same. Do you wanna fuck?" "Yes and No." I said and looked out the window, then back at him. "I feel that. You don't want me to think that you're a freak." He said turning down a street.

"I'm a freak. As a matter of fact I go both ways. I just don't want to hurt your feelings. Your pretty cool." I said as we turned into an apartment complex. "But if you really haven't had none yet, I'm going to fuck you to death!"

His apartment was nice and clean with freshness to it. We sat side by side on the couch smoking a blunt. He snatched his shirt off and looked so sexy with his chain on. I wanted to lick on his six-pack and chest.

"Nigga you think you da shit don't you?" I gave him a lustful grin. He walked in the kitchen and got something out of his refrigerator. I had my eyes on my manicure when he walked back in the room. I looked up to see him completely naked with a bottle of champagne in one hand and a handfull of Magnum condoms in the other. He threw them on the table and took a few gulps of champagne. His body was the definition of masculine and his dick had me leaking. It was hanging a good four inches on limp looking fat and chocolate.

"I want to talk for a second." He started. I gave him an expression that said I was listening. But his center was where my center of attention was. "You're a no good, low down, rotten as bitch! I know you don't mean a nigga any good! Yo pussy is a deadly weapon as is your mind. You can think. And quick at that, and will have a nigga in a fucked up situation, nothing personal, just business and you know what?" He took another swig of his champagne and handed it to me as I gave him the blunt. "Thank you! But you know what? You what I want, a rotten bitch, a bitch that don't stay in her feelings."

"Nigga that's what's up!" I said and got up and walked around the table and came out of my skirt and top and put his hand in my thong. "Nigga I can be whatever type of bitch you need for me to be. I can recognize a real nigga when I see one, nigga I saw it in you at first sight. Number one, don't put yo hands on me. I'll kill you. Two, fuck me good. Three, don't disrespect me…now. Give me some dick!" I demanded and got down on my knees to be face to face with my new toy. I grabbed his dick with both hands and kissed it. It instantly jumped hard as a pipe. I marveled at its new size and licked it from the base to its head. I couldn't take it any more and had to have it in my throat. I went crazy with his dick.

I looked up at him and ran my hand down his thighs, going at it with no hands. I came up for air licking my way up his stomach and chest. "Baby, yo dick taste so good! It's big too! Would you like for momma to make you feel good?" I asked as he busted a nut on the floor. I giggled.

"Damn!" OG said smiling from ear to ear. "Take them off." He said pointing to my thongs with his eyes. I called myself being sexy and wiggled slow and seductively and he snatched them off. He handed me a rubber. "Put that on." I did as I was told as he hit the blunt and blew me a charge then gave each of us a swallow of champagne. He sat both back on the table and picked me up by the ass and toted me to his bathroom. After bending me over the sink, he entered me from the back. I was so wet I could feel my juices running down my thighs. His dick felt so good as he was working his long stroke. Then he started playing with my clit. "Ah shit! Shit!

Shit!" I yelled as I came then shuddered. He kind of surprised me when he pulled my hair making me look at him.

"Girl yo pussy is good!" He said already sweating. I watched him fuck me from behind and felt another coming. Our eyes met in the mirror. "Your body is beautiful!" He said grinding harder but at a slower pace for some intense friction. He slapped my ass. "I wish you could see your ass from this shot!" he started biting softly on my back. I came again. He pulled his dick out and rubbed it up and down my ass crease. This time I took control and pulled him out of the bathroom and made him lie on the hall floor.

I got on top of him and sucked his shoulder. He squeezed my ass cheeks. I put him back in and rode him like my life depended on it. And it seems as if every time I tried to gain control and pussy whoop his ass, he pulls another stunt.

"Tell me that dick good girl I need to hear it." He says.

"It's good baby! Real good! "I said. It was all right.

"Naw. You're not feeling me. Tell me it's good girl!" OG said grabbing my hips forcing them to catch a rhythm with his. Hitting spots I didn't want him to touch. I felt another one coming.

"Ah shit! Damn! It's good nigga! Real good!" I said for real this time. "Ah shit! Boy I'm about to cum! Shit!"

"Cum for daddy girl!" He said then flipped me over on my back so fast it took a second to realize I was on it. He rubbed his dick up and down my fold and went back in. we caught a rhythm and both of us was grinding hard.

"I'm cumin baby! Shit! I... I...Shit!" I screamed and had an or-gasim. I knew then that I was way in over my head. It would be hard to set this nigga up.

Chapter 7
"Oil Can"

"What it is?" I answered my cell knowing who it was. "We got the nigga." Cool said. "Already." I hung up and jumped up out the bed to let off a piss. "Honey!" I yelled from the bedroom bath. "Get yo ass up and cook. Clean this mothafucker up or something!" I knew she was still mad from not getting fucked last night. I was mad from losing my car cause Lamira went to bullshitting like she was on her period. "Honey!" I got louder.

"Here I come!" she said in an aggravated tone. She appeared in the door with her face twisted up. "Girl you better fix yo mothafuckin face! Acting like you mad and shit!" I said giving her a look that said I wasn't in the mood.

"I'm alright," Honey pouted. "Now gone fix a nigga something to eat and why is you looking at my dick like that? My dick can't be that good to where you got to sit there and stare at the mothafucka!"

"Boy shut up!" Honey whined."

"Get yo freaky ass out of here!" I said and threw a toothbrush at her.

Honey had some pork chops, rice and gravy, biscuits, and a big glass of Kool-Aid when I got out the shower. I had lost my appetite from doing a line of cocaine in the shower. "Girl I done lost my appetite." I said apologetically. Honey dropped her spoon and gave me her screwface. "Nigga what?" She said while jumping in my face too quick.

"Girl you better get the fuck out my face!" I said with a shove. My cell rang. "What it is?"

"Say ole country ass nigga, I thought you were on yo way?" OG said as Honey got back in my face trying to pull my dick out of my pants.

"I am nigga, damn." I said and tried to move Honey's hands.

"Move!" She demanded, slapping my hands away.

"Where momma and Tiff?" I asked of his momma and baby momma. Honey had my dick in her mouth.

"They waiting on us at momma's. Nigga yo ass is probably still at the house?" OG said as I took Honey's scarf wrap off and ran my hand through her hair as she did her thing.

"Nigga I'm coming. In two different ways!" I hung up and looked down at Honey. She stopped and smiled.

"Shut up nigga. You know you wanted this like I did!" She said giving me her sexy look and kissed my man.

"Freaky bitch!" I said as she licked it like a lollipop.

"I love you too daddy!" Honey pledged and went to school with it.

"Nigga I'm telling you some real shit". OG was saying as I headed to the spot where Cool and Pimp were holding a dope phene and his bitch. They were eyewitness to an unsolved murder in, which a Trapstah Gangsta was in jail pending the charge.

"Nigga do what it do! Yes do that shit nigga. I'm going to fuck these hoes, and enjoy the benefits. Nigga I love these streets nigga. The Bluff baby! At the same my nigga, do you. You my nigga no matter what." I finished and gave him our handshake that had started with us.

We made it to Byrd Lake and parked in the dark parking lot. The woods were less than twenty feet away with a walking path going through it. I stepped out of the car as Cool slid open a van door. The interior light displayed the two faces of the dope phenes who were scared to death. I know their high had been blown being kidnapped at one of our dope spots and held at gunpoint until now.

"Yeah." I said remembering their faces on the scene when a Trapstah murked a nigga for being in the way. And the police were wheeling and dealing for eyewitnesses. "Handle that." I said as Cool nodded and pumped about five Tech nine bullets in the misses and then about the same in her man. Cool jumped out and went to dumping gas in the van as Pimp wiped down the door handles and glass. The van stood ablaze on the inside as I drove off in the Lincoln I was driving that belongs to the click. After dropping Cool and Pimp back off at their spot, I headed to momma's house in the hood.

OG's momma was my momma. And my momma was OG's momma. And I don't know whose momma is the worse. OG's momma, or Ms. Ann, stayed with her sister in the projects more than she stayed at home. OG's step daddy drove trucks and was never at home. So Ms Ann and her sister made money playing cards and talking shit.

"Took ya'll asses long enough!" she snapped at us talking fast as hell. She slapped both of us upside the head. "That girl got to go home to her man." Ms Ann said referring to Tiffany.

"Why do ya'll always got to be so slow?" Tiffany said sipping some wine with Ms Ann and looking at photos of Malicia.

"Momma. Why you ain't answer yo phone?" OG asked his momma frowning up at her. "I called yo ass four times. Don't be having me worried like that. My nerves bad enough already!"

"Alright boy, Damn!" Ms Ann said and then frowned at me cause I was about to say something. "Yes, I know yo ass called too, I seen your number in my phone a thousand times too! I was in the middle of some business!"

"All day!" I said frowning back at her. Ms Ann was pretty and had a nice shape. She was the cool mom. My real mom was a square.

"Boy, ya'll needs to get some business!" Ms Ann said and sipped her wine. We all sat down at the table in the kitchen and OG went to discussing what was on his mind.

"And third, Tiffany, I want you to start a non-profit organization. The Me-Me Foundation, I want you to take this thirty thousand and get it crunked up by next month. I'm giving you two more thousands for your services. I'll handle the rest. But back to the first, momma, we need that building. See what you can do. We got a hundred thousand to play with"

"Ooh!" Ms Ann said pulling on Tiffany arm like they were best friends. Her son and I spoiled her beyond reasoning. "Quit acting!" I said to her and Tiffany as they rolled their eyes in unison. "Fa real." OG said and went on. "We about to see this money in a major way. Momma, I want you to get ready to run some shit. So yo card playing days are going to slow down a little.

"I got you baby." Ms Ann said firing up a cigarette real feminine.

"And Tiffany I might have you some other businesses, or at least supervise them. But the foundation is yours." "OG picked the duffle bag up off the floor and dumped the hundred thousand on the table. "Let's turn this into a million and Lord knows whatever in assets. Let's get political and eat." He took champagne from his momma and sipped. He was choosing his words carefully as he eyed her suspiciously twirling the wine in the glass. "And momma yo ass is going to quit hiding shit from me too!" OG said upset cause she wasn't telling him something. "Already." I cosigned.

"You done found you a friend ain't cha?" OG asked her. She took her wine back and sipped while looking at Tiffany out the corner of her eyes. Tiffany dropped hers and then looked at her nails. OG adjusted his momma face so that she was looking in his eyes. "Why you ain't answer yo phone?"

"And come clean." I said eyeing her and Tiff.

"Ya'll so damn nosey!" Ms Ann said frowning.

"Momma!" I said demanding that she confess and she did. She was getting some dick on the side while the ole man was on the road. She knew her secret was safe with us and that we were not to tell the square mom.

"I want to meet this nigga." I said.

"Already." That was OG.

"Ya'll need to sit down somewhere." Tiffany put her two cents in. "Momma is grown and a woman has needs."

"Man, shut up!" I said and Tiff frowned.

"Fa real." OG cosigned.

Chapter 8
"Lamira"

"Yes bitch, and don't leave out any of the details!" I was telling Jaden as I was on my way to pick her up. We were making a trip to Pine Bluff to see the Piru niggas that wanted us to set up T.I and his partner.

"Stop and get me some gum and a bottle water." Jaden said and exhaled. We disconnected and I thought about my boyfriend Steve. The only reason I was with him because he didn't give a fuck what I did and he knew how to fuck me. I really didn't know if I liked pussy for real. Right now it was something new and it felt good. Steve was a compulsive gambler and would sometimes have money and sometimes be broke.

I kept him in the latest gear and gave him the Durango he drives.

I stopped at a Quickie Mart and got Jaden her items. The guy at the register tried to holla but I politely dissed his ass. I made it to Jaden's place and we were back on the highway giving each other the synopsis. Jaden gave me hers, crossing all T's and dotting all I's.

"Yes girl, the nigga sex game is on point. I got to let you check this one out! His dick is delicious, big and juicy!" Jaden said leaning back in her seat with her bare feet on the dash. She had a look of reminiscing.

"Girl, T.I look alike did a few lines, popped an X, smoked a blunt, and ran some of the tightest game I've ever heard!" I said switching lanes. "I played the period thing cause I was fucked up trying to hang with all those different drugs, and wouldn't have been in control, you catch me?" "I said with a side glance.

"Already!" Jaden concurred.

"N-E way, this shit might be harder than it look girl, these nigga's aren't no dummies." I said. "Yeah I know. This nigga OG had said that shit while I was on his couch and I thought he knew about us. I thought I was going to die." Jaden said and exhaled. "What are they paying you?" Well us?"

"Girl, I don't know! I mean, whenever I report an accomplishment, they break me off." I said as a diesel got beside me and made me nervous, I hated it when another vehicle that big was beside me. Jaden chuckled. "Shut up bitch!" I said.

"Bitch, I ain't laughing at yo scary ass! I'm thinking about how this nigga OG points his finger at nothing particular when he talked."

"Ah shit bitch, there you go already catching feelings!" I said as a warning.

"Bitch please, I just thought that shit was funny!" Jaden laughed out and turned the radio up as UGK's *"International Player's Anthem"* kicked on and we rapped in unison word for word.

⸻ ((●)) ⸻

Thirty minutes later we were in Pine Bluff in the hood of the East 7th Pirus. There were red outfits everywhere. Eyes and screwfaces made me slightly nervous as we got deeper into their concrete jungle. A motorcycle rolled up beside us so fast I jumped. The rider of the bike motioned for us to follow him. We turned a few corners until we was pulling up behind an Escalade parked in front of a small brick home. We walked along side a wide body black on black BMW in the driveway and a raggedy as truck in front of it. We entered through a side door and were punched in the nose by the weed smoke. Motorcycle man led us through the house as niggas stared and lusted grabbing their dicks. Jaden was unfazed by their actions and was looking at them just as crazy. That bitch was so bold and feared nothing. Sometimes I think her ass is a man in a female's anatomy. Probably why she likes pussy.

We ended up in a back room with two dudes that wanted her to pull this off.

"What it is?" Popcorn said. Popcorn had power and made things happen. He resembled a basketball player with his height and build. He had braids to the back. "Hey, what it is? Hey Demon. "I spoke. Demon was his right hand man and was down right evil, and ugly as hell. "This my BFF Jaden. Jaden, Popcorn and Demon. I trust her with my life." "Ya'll hoes daggin! I can see right through that shit." Demon said and went back to counting money.

"What? My dick wasn't good enough?" Popcorn said with his hand on his little print. What dick? His shit reminds me of an acorn. Not all tall men with big feet is packing. "What you got for me." Popcorn said sitting down in front of a chicken breast soaked with hot sauce.

"I got his number and has kicked it with him but them niggas are not dummies." I said.

"That's why I put you on that nigga. Slick as your ass is, it shouldn't take no time!" Popcorn smiled with greasy lips.

"My girl is kickin it with OG." I said and the room froze. Popcorn got up and got in my face standing over me with plenty of distance. "Say what?" Popcorn asked with a lot of interest.

"I'm fucking that nigga OG." Jaden said. Popcorn jumped in her face. Demon was looking evil as ever. "I can handle that nigga but it's going to take some time. All Lamira got to do is handle Oil Can which isn't as difficult as OG. "Jaden finished looking Popcorn in the eyes.

I could tell he was digging her. Jaden was fine as hell, plus she was gangsta.

"You see that!" Popcorn said looking back at me. He pointed at Jaden. "This bitch here is gangsta!" he turned to Jaden," Look, I want them niggas to fall! First I'mma steal their connect, then Imma smoke them niggas! Them pussy ass nigga's killed my brotha!" He got nose to nose with Jaden. "And I do not play no silly games shawty, handle you business, both of ya'll. "He walked over to Demon and counted out five thousand dollars and gave it to me. "That's for your previous services. Every time you come back with something, I got ya'll. Look, them nigga's money long but not like mine and if ya'll decide to play games?" Popcorn opened the door as two niggas toted someone in the room with a pillowcase over their head. The person had to have been a woman from her attire. She had on tight jeans and boots with a nice blouse. I recognized the dude taking off the pillowcase. It was motorcycle man, a very pretty girl appeared out of the pillowcase.

"Popcorn! Please! They lying! They lying Popcorn!" The girl was pleading as her make up ran down her eyes. Motorcycle man produced a gun with a silencer and put it at the base of her throat and let off two shots I barely heard. I let out a quick scream and jumped. Popcorn got back in my face. I saw the girl fall face first out my peripheral.

"Ya'll handle that bitness Ladies!" Demon spoke from the background still counting money, nonchalant of what just happened.

"My man hates that nigga OG. Bitch ass nigga killed our muthafuckin brotha! And if anything happens to that boy, the police will automatically look at us, which is bad for business." "Already." Popcorn said and went back to Jaden. "And that's the only reason the nigga still alive. So I say now. Handle ya bitness!" He opened the door and nodded sideways as if to say leave.

The car was quiet leaving Popcorn and Demon's example of what fucking up would get us. I was so far in my thoughts I ran a red light.

"Lamira." Jaden calmly stated my name. It was quiet again for a minute before she spoke again. "We might as well get on the job since we already in the Bluff. Gone and get us a room and fuck with these niggas!"

"Already." I said and got prepared to put my game face on.

We sat in our room talking on how we both keep seeing the look on ole girl's face, when Oil Can and OG finally showed up a few hours later. They were both fresh. Fresh hairdos, fresh fits, fresh kicks, and fresh diamonds.

"What it is?" Oil Can asked when I let them in.

"Hey Oil Can!." I softly smiled at him then spoke to his boy. "Hey OG!"

"What it is girl?" OG said smiling a nice smile. Jaden popped up. "What it is shawty? Damn!" He gave her a look over with his eyes that damn near made me melt.

"Hey Boo!" Jaden blushed. And I think it was a real blush. "What ya'll nigga got up?" Jaden asked looking like a model but thick with it.

"Shit! Ya'll called us!" Oil Can said and slammed down on the couch. He was frowning and reached into the pocket of his Sean John Jeans and pulled out a cell. OG had Jaden's attention as they stood by the door. I sat on the couch beside Oil Can. "Ay, what is that nigga stressing…hold on, what it is? Yeah the weather's lovely… yeah I'mma send a cool breeze your way. Already… I'm back nigga, ay, handle that." He hung up and sat the phone in his lap and rubbed his temples. He picked the phone back up.

"Nigga don't you see me sitting here?" I asked acting real cute. Thug niggas like feminine bitches with a twist of gangsta in them. "Nigga, I did't spend two hours on my hair for nothing. Check out my nails!" I put my nails in his hand. He still made his call with his right hand, but played with my hands with his left. He started conversing again but looked in my eyes as he handled his business. "Damn girl. I got shit moving. I didn't mean to be rude or nothing, come here, give a nigga a hug." He said and pulled me into a hug and he smelled so good.

"Damn you smell good!" I said by his neck loving the masculine fragrance.

"What type of games you playing?" He asked.

"What?" I asked real cute up in his face and got nervous by the question. "You up on nigga knowing you soft and beautiful, smelling like a cinnamon roll!" Oil Can said and touched my lip. I laughed a fake laugh to cover the relief.

"I bet you be telling all females that shit!" I said looking at his lips. "Girl I see something in you but I'm probably to gangsta for you. Get up." Oil Can said and it dawned on me that we was still hugging. He jumped up and snatched his shirt off. His chain hung to his stomach and he had tattoos everywhere. OG stepped in the room and was looking like a giant over Oil Can as he put Oil Can in a headlock.

"Let me go nigga!" Oil Can demanded.

"Nigga shut up!" OG said pushing him away. They went to shadow boxing with Oil Can holding his own. They were making that noise that dudes make when play boxing. Jaden came and sat beside me and we went to whispering. "Look at Oil Can's ass with those tattoo's!" Jaden whispered. "His ass is so sexy!"

"Let's fuck him together one day!" I said.

"I wonder how big his dick is?" Jaden smiled in my ear.

"What the fuck ya'll whispering about?" Oil Can said as we noticed that OG had came out of his shirt too. He was very muscled up and made a tingle go down my spine. I looked at Jaden's lusting ass and we met eyes and had the same thought.

"None of ya'll business!" I gave Oil Can a sexy screw face.

Ya'll got us fucked up!" Oil Can said with his mouth sparkling from his diamonds in his grill. He tapped OG on the arm. "You think she ready?" We were staring at each other.

"Nah, she ain't ready for you my nigga! She ain't ready for a Trapstah Gangsta!" OG said and they did their handshake.

"Already!" Oil Can said getting hype from his boy's encouragement.

"N-T-Ways!" Jaden and I said in unison. Oil Can went in his pocket and pulled out a small bag of cocaine he dipped his pinky with the nail on it and sniffed it.

"Ya'll come on, we bout to ride out." OG said. And it seemed, as if we automatically knew not to ask questions and do as we was told.

———◆———

Oil Can drove entirely too fast as we loaded up in OG's car. You Gotti had him feeling alert and on top of his game. We were going a good hundred, yet he handled the car to where you felt comfortable. I stared at Oil Can, making him look at me. I wiggled my bare freshly done toes. "Did I tell you that I liked girls too?" I said real feminine with a sideways stare.

"Oh snap! My girl got a girlfriend!" Oil Can said with a lustful glare.

"Yo girl?" I gave a sexy screwface. "Say nigga!" OG interrupted from the back seat with Jaden. "Nigga put that Rick Ross in, that Purple Codeine 6." Oil Can changed the disk. He slowed down and drove with his knee and did some more cocaine. He looked at me.

"What!" Oil Can ask. The moment was lost so I didn't want to press on the question I just asked him. I changed the subject.

"You look so sexy right now!" I said and turned and put a foot in his lap and felt what he was working with. He caressed it and went off in his thought as I did the same.

We shot to Memphis, Tennessee and went shopping. I always kept two thousands dollars on me cause I have an addiction. I love to shop. I also had the five thousand from the Pirus that Jaden and I had split. We had expensive shit, fewer bags. Oil Can and OG had expensive shit, with a gang of bags. Then they spent about two stacks a piece on us. Oil Can said that he wanted to see where my mind was.

"I want to play a game that will say a lot. All of us will buy something that cost less that a dollar to describe each other." He counted out four dollars and handed everybody one. "The best store for that is the Candy Isle. Buy it, put it in a bag, and hold it for later.

We left and went and got another room on Beale Street and ate some BBQ. We got off on Beale Street. The room was quiet while everyone devoured their BBQ. Shopping can bring on an astounding appetite. Jaden and I were on the couch while Oil Can and OG sat on the floor with their food between their legs. They seemed to always snatch their shirts off while they chilled, they could eat their Asses off too. We finished eating, cleaned up and rolled up two blunts of purple Cush weed and had a bottle of Cristal on ice. We all had our little game sacks and were now high as the clouds.

"So what did you get?" I asked Oil Can and gave him a quick look over. I rolled my eyes and then sat on my legs.

"I got you a Reece's cup! Because of your beautiful chocolate skin and that peanut butter outfit you rockin!" Oil Can said. I blushed before I knew it. Jaden saved me. "What did I get boo?" she asked OG.

"I got you an Almond Joy!" Cause when you get a taste of that Miami Sun, you yellow ass is going to be my *Almond* Joy!" OG said then jumped up and pulled her up to him. "What I get?"

"I got you a box of good and plenty cause your dick is good and plenty!" Jaden said and grabbed OG's dick through his pants.

"My shit is good and plenty too!" Oil Can said and had his long dick hanging out.

I just stared at it and knew right then that I was getting some of that. Jaden and OG were caught up in each other as Oil Can did a line of cocaine and popped an Extacy pill.

"What you gon' do with it when you get it?" He asked then sipped his bottle of champagne. "I'mma handle it papi!" I said to his dick. He walked it up to me and I grabbed it. I kissed it and then licked around it as he put an X pill in my mouth and a good swig of his champagne. He pulled me to him.

"I want you to know that you're fucking with a gangsta." Oil Can said sucking on my neck then my shoulder as he undressed me. I was down to my thong. I knew my curvaceous body was looking good. He bent me over the couch and sucked my pussy from the back. He had skills too.

He went to licking on my thighs while playing with my clit and squeezing my ass. That shit felt good! I came with a tremble. He poured some of the cold champagne down my ass and it made my pussy tingle. I started feeling the X pill and became super hot. My pussy started itching for his dick so I spun around and went to sucking it. I deep throated all I could and then went for his balls. I poured some champagne on them and sucked it off. I went back to licking and sucking with such intensity.

"Ah shit girl! Do that shit!" Oil Can threw his head back and grabbed my head. I looked in his eyes.

"Give me my cream filling baby!" I said playing with his balls and sucking with no hands. He shot off in my mouth and I kept going, licking on the sensitive parts.

"AAAHHH Shit! Damn! Girl!" Oil Can shout.

"Shut the fuck up in there!" OG yelled from the bedroom. Oil Can's dick was still a piece of wood as he slid on a rubber. He threw both of my legs on his left shoulder and slid in me giving me a good ten inches. He was grinding hard and touching things. He started long stroking.

"Oh my goodness! Damn this dick is good! Ooo oh shit! Oil Can! Oil Can!" I squealed as he pinched my nipples. He opened my legs and wrapped them around him and picked me up pinning me against the wall. I called his name over and over trying to encourage his ego but getting off at the same time. The next thing I knew he was pounding me from the back and pulling my hair talking cash shit.

"Imma keep you shawty! And you gonna get right too! I got to tame you wild ass!" He said playing with my clit. I came for the sixth time. We decided to take a break.

"So what you get me?" Oil Can said, doing another line. He chewed up another pill and took a swig of his drink. "What?" I wailed catching my breath. Right now I was in my after glow and he wasn't talking about nothing!

"The candy shawty." Oil Can said. We were standing face-to-face buck ass naked and he reached around me making one on my ass cheeks bounce up and down.

"I got you a Chico Stick and that should be self explanatory!" I said taking a sip of his champagne with both hands. I then caressed the tattoo 'Trapstah' and under it was 'Gangsta'. I kissed it and he picked me up under my ass and stuck his tongue in my navel. It was quiet and I could hear Jaden getting the fuck of her life.

"What's your Government?" I asked really feeling the Extacy and Crystal and rubbed my hands over his braids.

"Javon."

"That's it? Javon?"

"Javon Allen girl! Don't you see me trying to get my freak on?" He said in my belly button. Next thing we knew I was riding him. I felt a finger in my ass that some how felt good and made me cum instantly.

Oil Can seemed to never get tired and fucked me to sleep. I got up in the middle of the night to piss and my stuff was sore. That good pain I blushed from a good fucking and went curled right back in Oil Can's arms.

Chapter 9
"Tiffany"

It was a beautiful Saturday morning. I had just awoke in Neko's arms and was now just staring at him. We made love so strong last night. I felt rested. I thanked God for a good man and a beautiful daughter. What's really good is that I got a good relationship with her father. We're actually friends. I thanked God for making *me* a beautiful princess, of course, and got up and made Neko breakfast in bed.

"Thanks baby. That was proper. How you feeling?" Neko said looking sexy as ever. He was dark and tall with a handsome face. I loved his hands.

"I'm good!" I said soft and feminine. I was sitting on my legs on the bed beside him.

"What you think about the foundation?"

"I think that's some real shit. OG is a real nigga. It's a lot of niggas that respect that nigga in the streets." Neko said and drunk some of his orange juice "Ay and he love him some Malicia!" "Yes he does. N-E-way, momma and I got some shopping to do." I said referring to Ms.Ann. I put some hair behind my ear. "What time you coming home tonight?"

"Unno, why what it is?" Neko asked with his natural screw face.

"Nigga, I might want to be fucked real good again tonight!" I said with my "spoil me" voice. "Already shawty!" He said and wrapped me in his arms and it felt good being that my life was on point.

Ten minutes later he was gone and would be in them streets chasing money. Now I would be a damn fool to sit here and think that I'm the only woman he's fucking. I know he got his hoes but he respect me enough not to bring something home or let me catch him. I took a shower and went back into my thoughts. Next year I will be a Pharmacist and from what OG says and has planned, I will be able to pay all these loans off without hurting my pockets. I had trust in OG and his mind. He was a mean hustler. I would sneak him ounces of weed when he was on lock down and he would give me all the money he made. Every pamper Me-Me wore from day I brought her home had came from him. I had been with OG for only a year before he got locked up. We had separated two weeks before he left, cause his ass wouldn't stop cheating on me. A week after he was gone I found out I was pregnant.

I got fly as usual in a Baby Phat outfit with some cute Air Force Ones I found surfing the Net. I heard Ms Ann knocking on the door. I let her and Malicia in and ate a bowl of cereal.

"Is it cool out there?" I asked Ms Ann not able to tell by her attire.

"Kind of, sort of, I think it's nice!" Ms Ann said looking excited as she always does, even when she's mad. "Girl, we got some work to do!"

"What you mean *we*?" I asked.

"We Chile. Don't play with me!" Ms Ann commanded and kissed me on the forehead like I was her real daughter. That meant she missed me last week since we didn't see each other. She does OG the same way. "Your ass needs to start eating!"

"My man like it!" I said letting her know I got some last night.

"Girl, your man is crazy, I seen him staring at a midget!" Ms Ann said and we laughed at her crazy self. Malicia had ran straight to her room, probably counting and checking on them dolls, and was now standing next to me looking up at me with my eyes.

"Hey momma!" She said wrapping her arms around my waist.

"It took you long enough! How you gone speak to them before me?" I asked rubbing her chin kind of jealous of the dolls.

"Momma!" Malicia gave me a look as if telling me to be for real. "N-E-Way, I miss you momma, can I spend one more night at daddy's?"

"Yeah if you want to. What are you and your daddy doing?" I asked with curious arched eyes. Me-Me was too spoiled by her daddy and could get anything out of him.

"Nothing mommy, we watch CNN together and talk about life." Malicia said and smiled up at me. "He's putting his money on Obama!"

We were standing in front of OG's new business that was once a rim shop. Now it will be a detail shop with a gift shop for ballers cause he said that it would be selling everything. There was a big nice parking lot and they were already putting the name on the front along with a paint crew on the inside. *T.G. Detail.*

OG came and sat on the hood of is car while I leaned up against it with my arms crossed watching the crews work. Ms Ann, Me-Me, and Oil Can were in the way of the working crews by the front window.

"So what you think?" OG asked with a serious look. He was giving this his all. I now had the Me-Me Foundation up and running.

"Everything's good. I will put together a board and get things rolling." I said and looked at Malicia and thought about what she had said earlier. "Why you got my baby watching CNN?" I looked at his ass.

"We be on some real shit. We are on another level." OG looked at me seriously.

"Boy N-T-Way! What you been up too?" I asked and rubbed my arm.

"Not shit. Been on the internet getting shit ordered. I'm selling Lingerie, Teddy Bears, Calendars, Magazines, Music, Condoms, *everything!*" OG said getting hype cause now he was standing up and pointing his finger at nothing. "I got a whole bunch of shit in store for you ass too! Tiff, I'm telling you, we about to get paid! I just don't need them niggas fucking with me. I know they plotting and will try some shit. Only reason they haven't cause they getting money. And that my click will murk something with no talking about it!" He got quiet for a minute and looked at me for a second. "They'll probably try to use a broad to try to faze me. But I'm not going to be out there like that."

"Then get your girlfriend and sit down somewhere!" I said getting deeply concerned. "And don't move her in your apartment. We agreed to share Me-Me equally but amongst us."

"Damn girl, I know you, how you feel about me having another woman around your baby. "OG said irritated from constantly hearing it. "I been fucking with this girl named Jaden. She stays in Fayetteville."

"How did you meet?" I asked and hated that I felt a tinge of jealousy. "Through Oil."

"Oh snap! A real freak!" I expressed my assumption of this Ms Jaden. I looked at him and rolled my eyes.

"You already hatin." OG said. I smacked my lips.

"Don't get too serious. And, I want to check her out." I said with a quick side-glance.

"Why?"

"Cause I said so nigga, that's why!" I said and meant it.

"Man, we done been through this a thousand times! Now I respect your decisions, but don't be trying to run me." OG said now pointing that finger at me. I looked at him like he was crazy and decided to let it go.

"Yes, please, let it go." OG said reading me like a damn book.

"N-T-Ways! When are we up and running?" I asked and nodded my head towards the shop.

"A couple of weeks. What's up with your nigga?" OG finally asked. That meant he was still aiming to do what he told me when he made his towel do a disappearing act. That he was aiming to get me back. What his ass didn't know was that I never let him go. I'm just letting him get some new pussy until I find a way to fire Neko for his cheating ass. "Hey, I had a dream the other night." OG started, putting his arm around my neck and started walking us slowly toward the shop. "I was doing something…shit. I can't remember. But N-E-Ways, I got up and wanted to call you so bad! Like we used to do while you were at work." OG looked at me and put some hair behind my ear. "Member that?"

"Yeah. I miss our talks too." I said really missing them. OG use to call me at work and sometimes I would have to hang up in his face to keep from being caught or snitched on in my cubicle. We got tired of texting.

"Ay, Jaden is so fine!" OG said.

"So!" I said hating. I was caught off guard.

"But she ain't got shit on your fine ass! You know sooner or later I'mma tear that ass up don't you?" OG asked making me blush when I didn't want to.

"I hate your ass!" I said living in my compliment, smiling from ear to ear.

We made it to the building and went in and caught Ms Ann checking out one the painters who had on a tank top filled with muscles. Ms Ann was probably at home biting on his dark skin cause we startled her out of her thoughts.

"Have ya'll done lost ya'll minds!" She snapped from being interrupted. "Whew! N-T-Ways!" She eyed him one more time so fast only I knew she'd done it. She was trying to teach me how to do it. Malicia was watching the painting. "Baby I like this here!" Ms Ann said to OG. She looked at him about to say something but he beat her to the punch.

"No momma, momma you are not putting flowers and shit everywhere!" OG said and meant it. "Boy please!" Ms Ann said meant it. She also rolled her eyes. She had won and would have flowers everywhere.

———⊷«(○)»⊶———

Malicia was on the parking lot playing with her daddy while Ms Ann and I stood out side and caught up.

"So how old is this Teddy?" I asked Ms Ann.

"Twenty three!" Ms Ann whispered.

"Momma!" I gasped and looked at her like she was crazy.

"Girl, be quiet!" She snapped, talking fast like she could run an auction. She smoothly looked back at the painters making sure none could hear us. "I need something young, hell, I don't know what's wrong with me, but lately my pussy has been itching to be fucked and his young ass has been scratching it!" We giggled. I suddenly thought of something and it snatched the giggle away.

"How in the hell are we going to tell the guys?" I asked. OG and Oil Can would not allow her to be with a twenty three year old.

"First, shut up and let me finish," Ms Ann started and I gave her my look of approval. "I got and old school that I mess with too. He and I mess around a little bit, but he's nothing like my young gladiator! But N-T-Ways, the guys will meet him, and, I might let you meet my thug passion!" Ms. Ann said knowing she couldn't wait to let me give my approval. Her and I were tight like that. We had clicked from the very day I met her, when I told her I was pregnant with her son's child.

"When are you going to get your man?" Ms. Ann said speaking

of OG. "There's a lot of nookie a single man can get in the streets."

"Momma! Why you got to remind me, dang!" I looked at her and she said she was sorry with her eyes. "I'mma get him. He got to free himself right now. You already know that."

"Okay!" Ms. Ann said with her palms up. She was a beautiful woman. Her body was toned and shapely and I've never seen her with one hair out of place.

"Don't make me tell on yo ass!" I laughed out.

"I don't care! I'm grown! And sexy!" She said with a glamour look.

"OG!" I shouted.

"Girl, don't play with me!" Momma got back in check.

Chapter 10
"OG"

I was driving Oil Can's Cutlass on twenty fours. The paint was looking like syrup and the four twelve inch Kickers were living up to their name as I bumped *Plies*. I was cruising through UAPB passing out flyers and business cards. I had Jaden, Lamira and Oil Can doing the same in different towns. I turned the music down and changed it to Bobby Valentino making my way to the Hyper Building. College girls love them some Bobby Valentino. I took in the pretty faces as girls entered and left the building. I pulled in front on the entrance and parked. I left Bobby singing and passed out flyers and cards. I would be here five minutes or so and then move to another area on campus.

"Yes, damn near everything!" I was telling a girl with a drop-dead body with a funny looking smile. "Teddy bears, music, roses, clothing, all type of shit, you under me?"

"Already! Let me see that brochure." She said and I walked back to the Cutlass and raised up the Lamborghini door and retrieved a brochure I had made. The brochure had some girls that Oil Can knew modeling some of the Lingerie that I found at a bargain surfing the internet.

"What's your name?" I asked politely.

"Tanya. But most call me T!" She said with a cool persona.

"T, I'm OG. I like your style and would like to do some business with you. The first thing I noticed about you was your funny looking smile, which is now beautiful on you. It's yours! No one else has a smile like yours!" I said and she blushed like I expected then went for what was premeditated.

"I would like for you to model in one of my brochures. I'm also a photographer and would like to get you on a few projects. Now, right now, just think on it, and promise me you'll think on it. It will get you a free teddy bear!"

"Ooh okay!" Tanya smiled as I reached in the back seat again and got a Teddy bear. One of many that I had lined up. "He is so pretty, thanks!" She hugged her teddy bear. I did twelve more potential models for my calendars I was going to make.

I shot to The Pines Mall to layeth the macketh down. After four girls I got hungry and went to get a slice of pizza. When I finished my order a Latino honey pulled up with Gucci from head to toes to eyes. She was the terminology of pretty hot and tempting. I was staring and when she finished ordering I spoke my piece.

"Ay, let me handle that shawty." I said and she looked at me like I was crazy.

"I'm sorry, but I don't know you and I can handle my own." She said and rolled her eyes. She then handed the cashier her money and folded her arms.

"You are very beautiful!" I said with a big smile.

"I have a man, sorry!" She said with a fake smile and made it instantly turn into a look of being irritated.

"I didn't ask if you had one. Don't say nothing else, just listen." I started and she looked at me crazy. "I'm about to change your life. I'm a photographer and run a shop that sell calendars that I make." I pulled out my folded up brochure out my back pocket and opened it. "I want to create a business venture with you. You have model potential and a beautiful walk! Please, just think about it and let me pay for your lunch just for doing it. I'm trying to help you keep your money and make more!" I finished and smiled. She had to chuckle at my charisma. I gave her a card and she took it. We got our food and I watched her little sexy swagger as she walked off. If she looked back I was fucking her in two weeks.

Well, would you look at that! She did!

=»((◎))«=

Momma had the shop up and running. She would be running the register until she got some help. The customers at the present moment were females checking out the inventory. Momma use to manage a chain of boutiques and was handling things and talking to customers. I figured she was way too smart to be playing cards all day in the projects. The Detail Shop was ready but I had no cliental. My plan was to have all the ballers get their rides detail, and while they wait they could buy gifts for their girl, who's probably getting less of their time. The gifts they bought could be wrapped right there in the shop, even fresh roses where available. Plus the store will always have some Dimes shopping or looking, even if I got to *plant* them in the shop.

I would also be running a VIP section of the shop. The TG Club. I would be selling pictures, flicks, and documentaries. Momma didn't want any parts of that and would let me handle all aspects of that. When she finally stopped mingling she came over and tapped my arm. "Why are you over here staring at me?" Momma asked with a glow I wanted to know about. "What are you glowing about?" I asked with a curious look. "And you better keep it real momma." She asked and rolled her eyes at me.

"Why are you all in my flavor! Dang!" Momma said grabbing my hand and rocking it back and forth.

"I betcha Tiffany's ass know! You aren't going to tell Oil and me, ya'll probably got something already plotted! I know you slick ass momma!" I said and she fanned me off and joined two white girls that walked in, my ring tone kicked in. Jaden. "What's up stranger?"

"Nothing!" She sung feeling good I could now tell. We had seen each other and fucked a few times over the past month I had been out and she was real cool. She didn't sweat me.

"I was thinking about you the other day when I was passing out flyers." I said looking at momma making the girls laugh.

"And you say that to say what?" Jaden asked in her little innocent voice. "Miss yo ass shawty!" I said picturing her body. "Matter of fact, next time we fuck, we making love! Show you some Gangsta passion!"

"Already!" Jaden said sounding husky with a soft moan. "You won't believe what I'm doing!" "What you got going on over there shawty, what are you doing?" I asked in the voice I use when I'm hitting it from the back and pulling hair.

"I'm...I...I'm cuming! God! Oh God!" Jaden screamed, and if I weren't standing in front of the register, everybody would've seen my erection. She all of a sudden hung up as a cutie pie walked up to the register to make a purchase. I dropped the phone in my pocket and started scanning her items.

"Ay, how you doing beautiful?" I asked her not making eye contact to make her stare at me, only for me to catch her. "Fine! And you?" She said with a courteous smile. My phone vibrated letting me know I had a message. I flipped it open and discovered that Jaden had sent me some pics. One of her many fuck faces, and one of her bald headed fruit. I all of a sudden caught a whiff of her scent. I pushed the wrong button on the register and fucked ole girls' total up. "Damn!" I said trying to fix it. I apologized to her. "My bad. I didn't mean to cause any inconvenience but give me a minute."

To my surprise she stepped around the counter.

"Let me help you, I have this problem *too* sometimes." She said and hit some buttons and made it worse. Then she tried again and fixed it, and then set it to where it wouldn't do it again.

"Thanks! Ay, what's your name?" I asked bagging her stuff.

"Latunda!" she said with a white smile.

"Would you like a job here?" I asked. "We need some help right now and I think you're prefect for the job. Where do you work now?"

"Burger King." Latunda said with a I'm-kind-of-embarrassed smirk.

"Quit, and I'll hire you on the spot right now plus give you a dollar raise from what you was making, *and* a bunch of free shit!" I said making her laugh with her big pretty smile again. "WOW! I'll take it? Who are you?" She asked with a look of astonishment. "Your new boss!" I said with a confident look, flirting a little. "Nawl, fa real tho. I'm Octavious Green. Call me OG." I offered my hand and we shook.

"I really appreciate the job. I have been praying for a full time job for a minute now. Thank you so much!" She confessed with glossy eyes. I figured that the Eastside Pirus wasn't smart enough to get at a girl like this and felt that I could trust her enough to work here.

"What's your last name? Matter of fact, go ahead and fill your application out." I said and got one from under the counter. "I might as well introduce you to your manager who you're going to love!"

"He's not mean is he?" Latunda asked with her cute little nose.

"No *she's* not! She's incredible!" I said and led her to meet momma.

Wake you ass up nigga!" Cool shook me bringing me back from dozing off. I was at their spot waiting on Oil Can. I was high off the weed they were smoking and fell asleep because of the quietness.

I was back used to the noise of the world. I had raised Cool and Pimp, they had turned out to be some killers that knew how to chase money. The Trapstah Gangstas had a lot of enemies and was bringing that *a lot* into *too* many. I was going to clean up the click's money. I learned from Pimp C a long time ago that pimping was not dead, it just moved to the web sites. The click didn't know what I had in store but they were in for a surprise. I looked at my Rolex, and yawned. "Where the fuck is this nigga at?" I asked everybody.

There was also two fine ass females sitting on the couch next to me, in which was not here before I dozed off. The weed made me panic. "Who is ya'll?" I asked with a cold stare. "Were friends of them? Who are you?" one of them said after pointing at Cool.

"Bitch! That's OG!" Pimp said with his screw face. "Don't ever disrespect the Big Homie like that!"

"Dang Pimp, I didn't know!" She said like a little girl. Everybody got quite. I stared at the girls and they refused to look at me. A car pulled up and then came a knock in code.

"What it is?" Cool asked out from his seat on the floor.

"It's K-Dawg! Anytime, Any how!" the guy outside answered in code and was permitted in and purchased a nine piece, which was nine ounces and a few pounds of weed. I called Oil and cursed his ass smooth out. We were supposed to be on our way to Fayetteville to do Lamira's photo shoot. I received so many pictures in Prison that I stayed studying them and comparing them to magazines.

A vision came to mind. I now had a photo lab on my computer and ran a photo business at home. I had pictures of Malicia covering one wall in the guest bedroom turned studio. Oil Can finally showed up and I *had* to piss him off by punching on him and blowing his high. I was talking shit and we started pushing each other. Oil knew he couldn't fuck with me but I be damned if *another man* even try to put their hands on *my* little brother.

"OG, nigga, you got me fucked up nigga!" Oil Can said with a shove. His screw face was serious. I laughed in his face.

"Nigga, when I say be here at one, be here at one!" I said with my screw face, in his face. Cool got up and walked through us into the kitchen.

Him and Pimp was use to seeing us act like this. They knew that we weren't about to fight. Never that. But the girls on the couch were terrified.

"What the fuck ya'll looking at?" Oil Can said screw facing them.

"Come on nigga let's go!" I said grabbing his arm and he snatched it back. We screw faced each other. "I'll holla Trapstah." I said to Cool and Pimp and we was gone.

I was pushing the Vette at a hundred plus vibing and feeling Jeezy and DJ Drama mix tape. After we smoked a blunt together, which we rarely did, we were back Oil and OG.

"Nigga, this hoe Lamira is a real freak, you hear me?" Oil Can said out the blue. "Man that hoe let me punch in the ass! That shit feel good nigga!" He said in his light voice. "You wanna fuck that hoe my nigga?"

"Unno, I might. Right now we need to get these hoes up and running. I hope they aren't thinking that the dick is free, the shopping and shit! We gonna put these hoes on the web my nigga. "I said thinking of the big homies on lock down. "Imma sell this shit to prisons all over the state. Nigga we gone clean up all the click money." I finished passing the blunt.

"Already!" Oil Can affirm. "What's up with Tiff?"

"What it is?"

"What it *is*? Nigga you know what I'm talking bout. My mothafuckin sistah, yo girl!" Oil Can said as I slowed down for traffic.

"Man Unno." I said and meant. I wanted Tiff back to make us the family I wanted, but I wanted to explore my freedom for a while. "I hope she stays with that nigga Neko for right now cause I'm trying to fuck a few hoes before I settle down." I finished and sped up.

"That nigga's Neko isn't Gangsta enough for Tiff. That girl is crazy about you bro. She use to knock on my door at all times in the morning crying and shit. I damn near knocked Honey's ass out for trying to check her one night."

"What did she talk about?" I asked and Oil Can looked at me like I was stupid.

———◦《◦》◦———

We were sitting in Jaden's Condo with me on the laptop and Oil Can on the phone running The Trapstah Empire. Jaden's place was plush with white leather furniture and a stainless steel kitchen. This was where Lamira's photo shoot was currently taking place. My lighting was perfect but something wasn't right.

"Alright Lamira, change in that two piece Gucci and let's see how that reflect the light." I told her as Jaden was messing with Lamira's make-up and changing her hairstyle. This was the fifth change and it was a lot of work involved. I didn't have to push Lamira like a lot of the girls. After about the fourth change they get irritable easy. Everybody was ready as I adjusted the lighting.

Lamira was laid back on the couch with one leg hanging off. She had a baby oil shine looking like a chocolate eatable Barbie doll.

"We gone change the mood put that "Ay bay bay" on." I said as I climbed the ladder I had beside the couch getting a top view. "Now get comfortable Lamira, girl you looking good!" I said trying to motivate a sexy pose. She smiled up at me with sexy eyes.

"Work it girl! You looking good baby!" Jaden assisted me. Her and Lamira were *too close*. Like they are fucking each other type close.

"That's it Lamira! Girl yo body is banging!" I said and meant. She was rubbing on her self and making fuck faces. I some how caught an erection and broke a light sweat.

She came up to a sitting position and slowly wrapped her legs behind her head. I was snapping away as I watched through my camera staring at her camel toe. She was looking up at me lustfully which made Jaden look at me and spotted my erection.

"That's what's up!" Jaden smiled at Lamira. "You done made that nigga dick hard! You are going to have that effect on all niggas girl!" Jaden said as Lamira smiled and waved a pretty pedicure foot at me. Oil Can walked up finally off the phone.

"My nigga, I just might take you up on that offer!" I said the offer to fuck Lamira. "Already!" Oil Can said with his mouth imitating a chandelier from the lights hitting his grill. "Already!" I moaned out under my breath. This Dark Model with a gang of ass, hips, and healthy C cups had my mouth watery.

I loved this job. My ring tone kicked on. "Yeah?"

"May I speak to a Mr. Octavious Green?" a sexy too feminine voice asked which made me assume it was Tiffany playing games.

"Speaking, how may I help you?"

"This is Maria Cruz. I met you a couple days ago the Pizzeria at the mall. You gave me a business card."

"Yeah! Took you long enough! Everything all right?"

"Yes, I'm fine and you?" Maria asked with a clear Spanish accent. "Couldn't be better!" I said climbing down the ladder and standing in front of Jaden. I realized that we had never kissed. "Ay, I'm actually in the middle of a photo shoot. Can I invite you to lunch to discuss a proposition?"

"Sure! Name the place?"

"Fu Meigh's off Oliver street." I said looking at Jaden's lips that was perfect for her face. "Tomorrow at noon."

At Jaden's lips that was perfect for her face. "Tomorrow at noon."

"Okay, see you there!" Maria said and hung up.

"Got a date?" Jaden asked with her hands around my neck.

"Yeah, I met this Mexican girl in the mall the other day, a bad bitch, and I think we can use her."

"We?" Jaden asked.

"Hell yeah, we! I'mma let you run this aspect of a growing business!" I said and spun her around pressing my dick into her ass, girl look, we bout to build an empire, this photo business is just a small portion of what's going on. You are not getting the dick for free!" I said and she looked back at me like I was crazy. "I need for you to handle these hoes, cause if I handle them I'mma be fucking them which means less dick for you!" I said dry hunching.

"Maybe we can fuck them together!" Jaden recommended and pecked my lips.

"Already!"

Jaden said as we went into a deep French kiss. We broke it when it dawned on us that Oil Can and Lamira was right there on the couch fucking like Oil was out on furlough.

———※《◎》※———

I was riding shotgun while Jaden drove the Vette like she owned it. Fayetteville was snow bunny city and they loved them some chocolate. T-Pain was low on the radio as we cruised around with the top down. Summer was right around the corner and the weather was nice. Jaden was acting real girly and looking fly as usual. She was too gangsta for her looks though. You could easily mistake her for an army brat that's about to be come a prominent lawyer. Her face was so pretty and innocent. The braces. So I knew she had to be watched and could be dangerous. I never was the one to let beauty fool me. She pushed repeat on a song she was singing.

"Ay, don't be fuckin with the radio!" I said changing the song.

"Nigga I'm the one driving!" Jaden said.

"Then drive!"

"Nigga please!" Jaden expressed and changed it back. I looked at her crazy and she rolled her neck and gave me a crazy look back.

"Where in the hell are we going?" I asked rubbing the inside of Jaden thighs. She had on some Apple Bottoms so tight that they looked like paint.

"Somewhere special!" Jaden said driving with both hands at the bottom of the steering wheel. "I got to make a stop first."

"I'mma let you meet my other woman!" I said with a smile. "Malacia! Good, it's about time I meet the woman who gets more of your heart than I!" Jaden said with her bright smile.

"Awe, that so sweet! You got some real game!" I said of her statement.

"I'm fa real OG!" Jaden said looking at me with sincere eyes. I think she really meant it.

"Let's take our time and see how it plays out." I said with a peck on her neck, loving her scent. "Your perfume is the bomb!" I said and scratched her print between her legs.

"Just like you OG!" she said grabbing the back of my head with a hand.

"Why ya'll do that? I nibbled on her neck.

"What OG?"

"That! Say a nigga name all sexy, have a nigga trained with the calling of his name. I could be mad at yo mothafuckin ass, and you call a nigga name and, Blam! Ass whooping is set off until further noticed!" I said and it tickled tears out of her.

After stopping and getting some fresh fruit and a bottle of water, we went to a secluded spot in front of a lake surrounded by trees. It took ten minutes of dirt road to get here. We were sitting on the hood with a bottle of Cristal and a blunt of hydro. Jaden hopped in my lap and gave me a charge, then fed me a strawberry.

"Baby, I been itching for your dick all week, but I really need to be licked!" Jaden said sucking on my neck. She knew how to turn her freak on and off at the right time. She snatched my shirt off and then hers. She stood and inched her way out her tight as pants and was down to her thong. Her well-shaped legs were screaming for my touch. "Get naked." Jaden said. I was stuck for no reason. "Now nigga!" Jaden demanded with her hands on her hips. I abided. She ran her pretty foot up and down my stomach. "Remember my rules? Hmm? To fuck me good? OG I want you to fuck me good. Okay? Come taste me OG!" Jaden hypnotized as I eased up on her, gave her the blunt, and pulled her thong to the side and sucked her pearl tongue. "Shit! Hold up OG, I'm about to fall!" Jaden jumped from my skills. I used to make Tiffany beat the top of my head to make me stop. She sat down and I got on top of her.

"I need to let you know my rule!" I said licking on her Areoles and nibbling her hard nipples. My dick was hard and leaking precum on her stomach. "I run shit, you have *my* back!" I said and snatched her thong off and chewed her Jewel giving her two back to back.

"I'm ready for my lollipop OG!" Jaden said and we flipped positions. The only sound being heard was the birds, crickets, and the slurping of Jaden as she licked, caressed, kissed, and talked to my man. "Yes, I missed you so much!" she said to him and kissed him making the kissing sound.

"Damn shawty! You gone make a nigga think you're a boxer the way you giving me blows to the head!" I said looking at her pretty yellow face accentuating her short hairstyle. "Ha Ha very funny!" Jaden said with a cute smirk, and went to deep throating. I chewed some grapes.

"Ah shit! Suck that dick baby! Get yo prize girl get that prize! Oooh shit girl do that shit!" I said sipping some more Cristal as Jaden moaned and hummed on my stick. "Want some of this baby?" I asked referring to the Crissy.

"Pour some on my lollipop baby!" Jaden said with seductive eyes and smile. I poured some over my dick and she stuck her long tongue out and licked the inside of my thighs to my balls to the tip of my man again.

"Oh shit! Here come yo prize girl!" I gave Jaden her prize and she kept gong until she had swallowed every drop. The next thing we knew, Bun B's "Hold u down" was floating from the speakers, and we were standing at the trunk of the car with me hitting it from the back.

"OG! Oh ... shit! Fuck me OG! Fuck me. Ah shit!" Jaden moaned looking back at me with multiple sex faces. I started grinding and long stroking vigorously.

"Stop, Stop, Stop! Hold on! ...OG!" Jaden screamed and tried to run. I leaned on her back and reached under her and then played with her clit. "Aaah! Stop! ...I'm cumin! ...I'm cumin OG!" Jaden came. Her juices flowed down her thighs and I went down and licked them and then ate her from the back. She trembled and shuddered and came again. I spun her around and set her on the trunk. "Baby, you *always* beat the pussy up!" Jaden said with a giggle and a glow. She was beautiful. We went into a deep French kiss.

"Who the nigga baby!" I asked as Jaden wrapped her long legs around my waist. She was leaning back on the trunk. I fed her a strawberry.

"You the nigga baby!" Jaden saluted with a peck to the lips. "Number one Trapstah Gangsta! Which means I'm the number one Trapstah Queen!" She kissed my Trapstah House Tattoo on my chest. "Already!" I said with an idea floating around in my head.

Chapter 11
"Lamira"

I awoke with the damnest headache. It took me a minute to realize that I was still at Jaden's condo. I looked behind me and saw Oil's diamonds glistening through his open mouth. Flashes of the rough and fantastic fucking he put on my ass last night had a tingle back in my love box. My stuff was sore with that good pain again. I woke his ass up.

"Baby, get up." I whined rubbing on his dick.

"What it is? What time is it? Where OG?"

"Nigga slow down! Damn!" I said going down on him.

I damn near made his toe nails pop off. I got up and made him breakfast chops, rice and gravy, butter rolls, and a bottle of Cristal. Oil Can took his grill out, and then ate.

"Where my brotha?" Oil Can asked eating his food like he just got out of prison, and *then* he was making a mess.

"Him and Jaden went somewhere yesterday, so it really ain't no telling." I said leaning against the counter in a panty and tank top set that said My Reality Check Bounced. Oil Can was making me feel naked the way his eyes roamed my body, making me tingle. "Dang! Didn't you get enough? My stuff is sore!" I said walking up on him cupping his face. He palmed my ass as I pecked him.

"Did you do what OG told you?" Oil Can asked feeling on my titties like he had never felt any. "Yes, I sent all the big homies money orders and the flicks ya'll took." I said messing with his eye brows.

"Ay, my nigga wants to hit." Oil Can said.

"Oil Can!"

"Girl, you know you wanna fuck my nigga!" Oil Can said with a smile. As hard as I tried not to, I blushed. OG was a *sexy ass man*! He made me feel so confident and free during the photo shoot. Plus Jaden says his sex game is tight.

"Is that what you want?" I asked as his ring tone kicked on.

"What it is?" he asked and then frowned. "Honey! What the fuck I tell you? You're a hard headed mothafucka! I'm kickin yo ass!" He hung up. "Bitch done wrecked my Chevy!"

***

I drove to Little Rock while Oil Can talked on the phone, constantly licking his lips. He kept the volume of the radio at a level to where you couldn't hear what he was saying, and then turned it off when he was through. He was obviously mad about the Chevy that some girl named Honey had wrecked. We made it to his apartment and he flat out paid me no attention. I oddly felt unattracted as he talked on his phone, snorting cocaine, and turned the television like he was crazy. Sometimes he would jump up and go to talking crazy to who ever was on the other end. I stared at all his tattoos on his shirtless body. He had changed his chain hanging around his neck and was now rocking that same house that was on his chest.

"Lamira!" Oil can called out with his back to me.

"I'm right here." I eased up behind him and purred in his ear. "You aight?"

"Shit Nawl!" he said turning to face me looking like he could snap at any moment. He had broke a light sweat. "Roll me a blunt." He demanded and got back on the phone. I did as told plus gave him a bottle of champagne out of the fridge. Since he paid me no attention, I started probing around. One thing that stood out to me was that there was not one photo in the house. Nor any sign of a women staying here. All the closets were full of clothes and shoes. The apartment was neat and clean with little furniture. I was pretty sure he didn't actually stay there. When I went back into the living room Oil Can was on the phone with OG.

"Why didn't you tell me that shit yesterday? Man, I might not make it… nigga fuck that!

I'm the one handling all the business nigga while you on that positive shit! Niggas is dying and the Trapstah click is on the rise!" Oil Can said motioning for me to give him a light. "Niggas is snitching, bitches are getting niggas set up! I be glad when yo ass turn back to OG!" Oil Can said in a tone which scared the shit out of me. It was as if he knew something. I wanted to say *you can trust me* but that was my conscience. He went in a duffle bag now sitting on the table and pulled out stacks of money, stacking it on the table. "Yeah she with me…Aight…Aight… I said Aight nigga!" He hung up. "Ay, we got to change clothes and since you don't have none we going shopping. Roll me another blunt, fix me up a line, and a shot of Pa'tron. What the fuck you looking at me fa! Now!" Oil Can startled me and it kind of turned me on. His authority had a helluva presence. I felt a tingle between my legs as I did as I was told.

After leaving University Mall we shot to Pine Bluff in, which automatically made me think of the Eastside Pirus. It wouldn't be long before all this would come to an end. I would be back boosting clothes and tricking with ballers. It had been a while since Jaden and I had done something sexually, hell, we barely had time for our talks.

OG had *both* of us busy. In the end, someone would have to die and it wasn't going to be me. All I had to do was relay information until the Eastside Pirus was satisfied and then Jaden and I were out. I was starting to like Oil Can and his friend, but business is business.

We made it to the Bluff and met Jaden and OG at the Convention center. I had on a black strapless Vera Wang dress, diamonds, and Stilettos. Jaden was similar while Oil Can and OG had on black Tuxedos. We were standing in the parking lot at the trunk of Oil Can's Vette. "Everybody on point?" OG asked Oil Can.

"Already." Oil Can said looking around the parking lot, then at me. "What?" I nervously asked and looked at Jaden for support.

"Just thinking, that's all." Oil Can turned to Jaden. "Next time you decide to leave with my brotha, make sure you call me."

"Yes father!" OG meddled. Oil Can gave him a look and OG fanned him off.

We were attending a fund raiser for the ME-ME Foundation and everybody had on black. I had recognized most of the men that was serving champagne as Trapstah members from the party a while back. Jaden and I had seats up front while Oil Can and OG were hosts. Things got started and a woman named Tiffany Powell informed us of what the ME-ME Foundation was about. "We will also be providing afterschool programs for disruptive teens." She said as everyone clapped. Ms. Tiffany was so pretty that she looked fake. Like a porcelain doll. I wondered if OG or Oil Can had ever fucked her. Oil Can was now in front of the podium smiling, now with white teeth.

"Now coming forward with a donation, representing White and Lowery Law Firm, Miss. Lamira Lawson!" Oil Can said with open arms for me to come up.

"Thank you Mr. Allen!" I said once I made it to the podium. I smiled. "We at White and Lowery see the Me-Me Foundation as a light house for those in aid, those who are troubled, and those who just simply care!" a soft clap went through the crowd and I finished what OG had prewritten for me. "With that being said, our firm proudly donates ten thousand dollars to the Me-Me Foundation!" I smiled as cameras went off and then turned to my left to see a big ass check like the ones on TV.

I felt like I was in a dream or something. What the hell was going on? Now I *knew* I was in way over my head. This nigga OG was about to be a force to be reckoned with. He was cleaning up dirty money with professional help. He was paying people to donate as tax write-offs but giving them their money back with interest, and turning dirty money into legit currency. Seven other people, white and black came up and did as I. some with more, some with less. There had to be at least ten Trapstah members taking pictures, mines was taken five times already. You can now make that six. Everybody was now mingling as Jaden and I went into one of our watch-the-crowd-and-talk sessions.

"Girl, what the hell is going on?" Jaden asked what I wanted to ask.

"Girl, unno!" I said looking around. OG and Oil Can were talking to the porcelain doll and an older woman. They all seemed to be enjoying each other. "You see that?" I asked Jaden on their enjoyment.

"mm hmm!" Jaden said and sipped her champagne.

"This nigga Oil Can asked me did I want to fuck OG this morning!" I said really wanting to know Jaden's output of the situation.

"Do you want to?" Jaden asked and I gave her a look that said yes I would love too! "Then fuck him girl, want me to set it up?"

"Nawl, girl I'm tripping, let's handle this business." I said and sipped my champagne.

"And get a good fuck out of the deal! Girl the nigga got skills!" Jaden said making me spit a little champagne out my mouth. "What? We might as well pull a ménage on his ass!" She purred out.

"Already!" I sung out.

The fund raiser was over and everyone was mingling before we left for the afterparty. Jaden and I was standing at the entrance when Oil Can and OG strolled up laughing with the porcelain doll and the older woman, who now looks as if she could be OG's mom.

"Ay, Lamira, this is my sistah and my momma." Oil Can said pointing at them.

"I'm Tiffany and this is Ms. Ann." Tiffany said and tapped Oil Can upside his head. "How ya'll doing?"

"Oh were good! This was such a nice event!" I said and realized I hadn't introduced us. "Oh I'm Lamira and this is my BFF Jaden!" I extended my hand.

"Jaden... I've heard that name before." Tiffany said shaking my hand but looking at Jaden. "That's the Jaden I spoke of." OG said and wrapped his arms around Jaden. "Jaden this is Tiffany, my baby's mother."

"Ya'll look nice together, you go girl!" Tiffany smiled at Jaden. But female instinct told me she didn't like it.

"Call me ASAP!" Ms.Ann said to Jaden. She was wearing very clear skin and a figure to die for. "Momma! Honey wrecked my Chevy!" Oil Can interrupted, relieving us of the oddness.

"The one on twenty fours?" Ms. Ann asked looking as if it was her favorite. "Dang! Is she alright?" That was Tiffany.

"Yeah she straight, just hard headed!" Oil Can said licking his lips. "What ya'll bout to do?" He asked Ms. Ann and Tiffany.

"Can we come to the after party?" Ms. Ann asked. "No!" Oil Can and OG said in unison.

<hr />

We went to another one of Oil Can places and changed clothes. The girl named Honey was here in a back room.

"I'm in here!" She answered when Oil Can called out for her.

Him and OG were Already shirtless. Oil Can went to her and commenced to beating her ass. OG sat down at the bar and took out his phone and started texting. The girl in the room was screaming and yelling. Jaden and I gave each other the better-her-than-me look. All of a sudden the girl ran from the back, passing us with nothing but a thong on, and went into the kitchen. She grabbed a knife and ran back towards Oil Can. He side stepped as she swung and knocked her completely out. He dragged her up against the wall and sat her up. He took the knife back into the kitchen and came back with a pitcher of ice water. He threw it in her face.

"Wake up you stupid bitch!" Oil Can said to her and she came back to life in a panic. She looked at us and then at Oil Can.

"Why you doing me like this? I told you I came on my period and didn't have any pads and my momma got my truck!"" Honey yelledd with perfectly arched eyebrows. She was pretty even in the predicament she was in.

"Bitch! I don't give a fuck!" Oil Can started with an evil, mean, tone. "I told yo stupid ass not to fuck with them cars period! You so fuckin stupid! Bitch, you don't pay no bills, you laying up in my shit, I constantly buy you shit and you can't follow simple fuckin instructions," he kicked her in her ass and she balled up and cried. "Now I got to go report my shit stolen you stupid bitch! You better pray they don't search it, you know why bitch! Tell her why OG!"

"Cause the car is full of dope!" OG said and shook his head. "Stupid ass bitch! My nigga told you over and over not to fuck with the cars!" OG was just as mad.

"Bitch, get the fuck out! Now!" Oil Can shouted with his screw face.

"I need to put on some- Honey tried to plea."

"Bitch you think I'm playing don't you?" Oil Can said under his breath and started punching her. He grabbed her hair and dragged her out the door.

"I'mma pay somebody to *fuck you up*!" Honey shouted and took off running in her thong. Oil Can took off after her. OG walked up on Jaden and I.

"Look at my baby!" He said showing us a picture of a little girl in his phone.

"Wow! She's beautiful!" Jaden said. I had my mind on Honey. She was being chased in a thong. Ten minutes later Oil Can came back through the door.

"You must've forgot that bitch was a track star!" OG said and chuckled. Oil Can took his time and sat down.

"Lamira! pack up her shit and bring it in here. When you finish, cut it *all* up!" Oil Can said and did a line. "Fuck you standing there for Jaden, give her a hand!"

"Already!" OG cosigned.

I was in the back of a suburban with TV's everywhere. Oil Can and I were cuddled up watching American Gangster. OG was driving with Jaden shot gun. Two guys named Cool and Pimp were riding along. My hands were extremely sore from cutting up all Honey's stuff. Jaden and I must've cut up at least twenty thousand dollars worth of clothes and purses. Her shoe game was another story as Oil Can and OG watched us and got high. We were on our way to club *Twenty four*, for the after party and the atmosphere of the suburban was comfortable.

"What's on your mind?" I softly spoke into Oil Can's ear, rubbing the back of his head. "Cause I know its not the movie. you aight?"

"Shit girl, I'm higher than elephant nuts, ya dig?" Oil Can smiled, mouth blinging now with yellow diamonds. I looked out at the cars we were passing then back at him.

"Kiss me." I said seriously and he looked at me like I was crazy.

So I took it and made him kiss me and it got good. The next thing I knew I was as hot as a red chili pepper and what do you know, my phone vibrates and bring me to my senses in which I didn't care to be at that moment. That shit felt good! "Hello?" I said with a sexy screw face at Oil Can with my finger in his mouth, with now me now laying across his lap.

"What it is?" The other end said and my heart fell into my stomach. It was Popcorn, from the Eastside Piru's. If I had not been high and tipsy, I probably would've panicked. I some how managed to stay calm and thought of something.

"Hey momma!" I said smiling and gently eased my finger out of Oil Can's mouth.

"Slick Ass." Popcorn chuckled. I appreciated now more than ever that he was soft spoken cause the movie wasn't loud at all. "What you got going?"

"Oh I'm good! Making real progress. I've come along way momma. Jaden's here, were with some friends!" I said as calm as I could looking at Oil Can, caressing his face.

"That's your momma?" Jaden asked from up front.

"Yeah, she says hey!" I lied. Oil Can squeezed my C cups.

"So I take it you got something for me and I'll be seeing you soon?" Popcorn said. It sounded like a porno movie was going on in his background. I broke a slight sweat under my arms. "Yeah, I'll be to see you tomorrow!" I said nervous and improper. "Where's that nigga OG? Popcorn asked. "Oh, she's up there in the passenger seat, she said hi back." I said and Jaden knew that some slick shit was going on cause me and my momma do *not* get along. Nor does she like Jaden.

"Good! Come see me Sunday." Popcorn said and hung up. Damn. That was *too* close for comfort.

Chapter 12
"Tiffany"

I was mad. I had planned on coming home and raping Neko while I thought about OG, but this nigga had wrapped his arms around that girl he *barely* knew. Okay I'm hating, so what? Neko was on top of me doing his thing but I was doing a poor job faking it cause he pulled out of me, cursed me out and left. I set up shop on the couch and made Me-Me get up out her sleep to join me. She had been with OG all week, *and then* they stayed on the phone.

"Seasoning salt?" I asked her from the kitchen. I was making popcorn. "No! Daddy says salt will have my blood pressure high. Hot sauce like yours mommy." Malicia said looking grown on the sofa flipping through channels. "You and your daddy is a hot mess!" I sat on my legs beside her. Webbie's "Independent" video came on the TV and we sung it word for word in unison. I heard Neko's sound system over the TV as it had the furniture shaking. He came in looking crazy and walking fast."Neko!" I got up and followed him in the bedroom. He had left his car running with that shit still loud. "Why you got that music up like that! You know how these people"

"Girl, get back!" Neko yelled with his screwed face. "I'm on something else right now!" He went into the closet and I knew what he was getting. I seen the print of it on his waist when he came back out.

"Why you get your gun?" I asked. Somebody please tell me why do gangstas sag their pants with their gun because I don't know.

"Tiffany, go on now, I got to handle something." Neko said trying to walk by me. I jumped in his face.

"Nigga you better talk to me!" I said with my screw face. I'm not some hoe you fuck, I'm your woman!"

"Man, gone!" Neko said getting agitated.

"Man fuck you!" I mumbled under my breath, went and got back on the couch. "With yo nosey ass!" I said to Me-Me because she had muted the TV, not missins a beat. My furniture stopped shaking as Neko Left.

"Momma."

"What?" I said dryly. I had lost my mood of relaxation. "What's wrong?" Malicia asked with the same concerned eyes I see in the mirror sometimes."What'swrong with what?" I asked looking at my baby.

"With you and dad?" Malicia asked playing with my nails.

"Who?" she took me by suprise; I thought she was referring to me and Neko.

"Dad! Daddy! OG! Octavious Green! Duh!" Malicia smirked.

"Girl, Octavious and I are friends. Now, I didn't say I didn't miss and love him, we'll eventually get right." I said unmuting the TV. Malicia took the remote and hit mute again.

"Grandma says that your letting him clean out his closet!" Malicia said cheesing and chuckling. I smirked. "Let's call him!" "Ain't!" I playfully frowned.

"Your scared of daddy! I see the looks that yall give each other. Yall love each other!" Malicia stated with innocense.

"Girl, what do you know about *love*? Describe *love*?" I asked.

"You and daddy!"

———◦((◦))◦———

Me-Me half tricked me into calling him. The other half was on my own. I needed his friendship right now. He came and scooped us up for lunch at Mickey D's.

"I don't like Jaden." I said eating a fry.

"Don't hate!" OG said with his signature smile.

"I mean, she's *beautiful*! But I see some slickness behind it." I said kind of enveying her.

"Not as beautiful as you Tiff!" OG said knowing exactly what I wanted to hear. He rubbed my face.

"Who's Jaden?" Malicia asked sipping her soda.

"His girlfriend!" I said sacarstically.

"And when will I meet her?" Malicia asked looking at neither of us.

"Never!" I said at the same time OG said "soon!" We looked at each other, I rolled my eyes. Me-Me did the same.

"What's up with Neko?" OG asked.

"Not shit. He swear he's the shit and is about to get fired!" I ate another fry.

"Damn." OG said pulling his straw in and out the lid.

"N-T-ways!" Malicia interupted. "Mommy, Daddy, I will be f-i-v-e next week!" She looked at me then at OG. "Can I have a cell phone please?" She asked as fast as she could with pleading eyes. She stole that move from me.

"No!" I said at the same time OG said"Sure!"

"Girl what do you need with a phone?" I asked cause I knew OG would give her spoiled ass one anyway.

"Cause momma, you always get mad when daddy call me on your phone." Malicia snitched. I would also get jealous. I wanted him calling me. Malicia's ass was way too grown for her age but was a good child. She's incredibly obedient and is very smart for her age. "Me-Me, you are not getting a phone." I said with my look.

"Yes mamm." She said and accepted her lost. "Ay, and back to Ms. Jaden, remember what I said?" I said pissing OG off.

"You know what? I'm moving her in first thing tomorrow since you can't leave that alone." OG said with a screw face.

"And Me-Me will never step a foot in there as long as she's there!" I said with mine.

"You got me messed up! Who you playing with TIff?"

"I am not playing."

"Momma! Daddy! Dang! Ya'll making a scene!" Malicia said making us gather ourselves.

I rolled my eyes at OG. At that moment I couldn't stand him.

"N-E-way, you shouldn't do that." OG said leaning his elbows on the table.

"Shouldn't do what OG?" I asked with my arms folded across my chest. I was ready to check his ass.

"That?"

"That what?"

"That bullshit, that you doing now!" OG said to my face.

"Nigga fuck you! I mumbled back OG and gave me an 'I'm-not-playing look.

"We are acting like children here!" Malicia whisper yelled at us.

"Man be quiet!" OG said to Malicia with his screw face.

"Fa real!" I gave her mine. She threw her hands up and gave us a I'm-out-of-it expression. We shared a laugh. It was a wander to me how we had created a life through our love making, and for helping me create something so beautiful, at that moment, I loved him.

"You know I"m telling momma on your ass!" I said to him. I just had t o have the last word.

A week later I was at the shop talking with Ms.Ann. I couldn't wait to tell her of the conversation me and OG had, we lived for each other's opinion.

"He had the nerves to tell me she was moving in!" I said and almost forgot I was in the store with customers cause Ms.Ann had done the same. She was with a customer when I had came in. Now we were off in our own little world.

"She does look slick." Ms.Ann said. "And is very pretty."

"Momma." I gave her my don't-rub-it-in look.

"Okay, she's nice looking!" She said putting some Lingerie on the right rack. The store was busy with customers. OG had hit it right on the money with the store and detail shop. The car wash was busy at the moment with mail trucks. OG had a contract with the postal service along with other companies.

"We have to watch her momma!" I said helping her organize the rack.

"Already!" Ms.Ann said anticipating to talk about her young love.

"Dang!" What has Teddy done now?" I asked and as expected, she couldn't wait to tell me.

"Girl, he stuck an Ex pill in my ass!" Ms.Ann whispered.

"In your coochie!" I asked.

"In my *ass!*"

"Ooh!" I said breaking a sweat. OG had introduced me to Extacy pills. They made fire crackers go off in the bedroom.

"Girl, that boy fucked me to death!" Ms.Ann said rolling her eyes and fanning her beautiful brown self,giggling like a little girl. "It would've been easier for me to have had another child that to have been taking all that dick to the early mourn! You catch me?

"Already!" I agreed, envying that her sex life was good. I mourned for some good dick. Ms.Ann had to go back to the customers and I mingled, checking out the new stuff. OG's foundation had me busy with the little spare time I had while, he kept Malicia off my hands. I was handling fifty thousand dollars from just one event, and I've seen a list of ten more. If this Jaden girl catch wind of the money that OG will be worth, she'll ruin my plans of getting my man back. A couple of fake thugs with fake grills tried to holla at me but being the lady I am, I politely dissed them. Bad as I wanted to, I didn't cheat on my man. Neko was starting to get on my nerves. I hadn't been fucked good in a month. I bet Ms.Jaden is getting the ride of her life cause OG had skills. I use to get off just as easy from thinking of the love we use to make. Now those memories are too old and needs refreshing.

Chapter 13

"OG"

A trapstah Gangsta had been murdered, and when I first heard it, it took me off my positive horse and made me realize that I was still surrounded by negative stallions. I knew Oil Can would not let this die easy. *I* wasn't going to let it die off easy. Every member of the Trapstah Gangsta click had a bond for each other. Since day one we gathered twice a week to discuss business and issues. Everything that a Trapstah did was reported. We were down to eighty six members. I wanted to turn the other cheek for business purposes, but the click looked up to me and Oil's decisions. That meant somebody had to die. I *really* didn't want to be around Oil right now cause my friend can get *real* ignorant. We were at Janon G's furneral not enjoying it nor relaxed. Soldiers were on post outside and when it was their time to view the body, they were relieved of their post. Every Trapstah gave Janon's momma a hundred dollars and we left and had a meeting.

"I don't give a fuck my nigga, we can hit every hood around this bitch!" Oil Can said to the click. We were in Humphrey, Arkansas in the middle of a field with two double wide trailers.

"I heard that Janon G was at Sam's playing pool last night and two niggas approached him." One Trapstah member named Otis said. "This was before he got shot. Now, some hoes told Pimp that the two niggas had on hats with 'Loot or Die' on them."

My heart sunk.

"Loot Niggas?" I asked referring to The Loot Dawgs. They were a click that was twice as deep on the westside of The Bluff. "Damn! Any mothafucka care to tell me some shit?" I said heated. I recieved screw faces for answers.

"Nigga we just as fucked up!" Omar said with sincerity. He had been with the click since day one.

"Let's handle it OG! It's all on you!" Cool said and meant and I hated it the moment he said it. Since I had been gone Oil had been running the click and had done what he had to do to hold it down, with or without my decisions.

"Whatever Oil want to do, I'm riding with that!" I said and gave Oil my look of approval. "Already!" was said all through the crowd.

⟫⟪◍⟫⟪

Two hours later I was stretched out on my couch watching CNN with Malicia.

"Daddy what is war?" Malicia asked as we watched troops in Iraq carrying kids caught in an explosion.

"Unneccessary violence." I said rubbing my hands through her long hair. She was laying on my chest. "Like you and momma?"

"Me-Me, why would you say that?" I asked cause her words had touched something.

"Violence hurts doesn't it? It hurts me to see you and mom not together." Malicia said enjoying her scalp massage.

"I love your mother, I respect her and her decisions, but she has a boyfriend and I got a girlfriend. We're good friends Me-Me, and that's better than anything in the world. Don't ever lose a good friend, ya hear me?" I said and twisted hair around my index finger.

"Yes sir. But daddy, momma is *always* talking about you!" Malicia said and I could feel her smile even though I couldn't see it. She looked up at me and there it was.

"I betcha you be telling her I be talking bout her all the time?" I asked with a smirk.

"I do not!"

"That's my girl!" I saluted with a kiss on her forehead.

"Ooh daddy look! There goes your man!" Malicia said referring to Obama on the TV.

"*My man!*" I said like Denzel in American Gangster.

It was a nice day so I dropped the top on Oil Can's Vette with Malicia riding shot gun. We bobbed our heads to Rich Boy's cd as we cruised the city. So many new thugs had sprouted as they rode the main streets instead the back ones. I knew the streets knew I was out cause my click was deep in the streets and was reppin me. My buiness was booming and I had a lot more in store. I was coming down 28th and made a right on Olive Street and caught an idea.

"Say nigga, this is what it is." I started telling Oil Can after calling him. "I want us to get a Candy Purple Hummer H3 on some twenty eights. Advertising The Detail Shop."

"Already. Where you at?" Oil Can asked.

"Riding with Me-Me." "Tell her I got her gift and I'll holla at her tomorrow." Oil Can said. They had also accomplished a relationship in the last four years, and we are the *only* two men she's allowed to trust. I delivered the message and she gave me a thumbs up.

The shop was alive with customers as momma and Latunda ran the registers like professionals. Pretty girls were everywhere as businessmen and ballers lusted. Some of the girls were planted as eye candy, and I've come to find out that there's plenty of lesbians in Pine Bluff.

"Busy day?" I asked Latunda as I came behind the counter with Malicia on my heels. "Extremely!" She claimed smiling as usual. She had become an asset. She was unbelievably smart and had alot of patience. She could deal with difficult, dumb customers. "Your brother called and told me to ask what color again. Hey Me-Me!" She bent down and hugged Malicia. I called Oil Can.

"Purple." I said and hung up. "I'm bout to get us a Hummer!" I looked at momma. "On some twenty eights!" I said to my ever so beautiful mother. She loved her rims. I kissed her forehead and caressed the back of her ears as she rung up a pretty cutomer's purchase. Most girls came and bought their own shit.

"Already!" Momma said looking young enough to be asked for an ID. She was still my number one girl. She loved me regaurdless, in all my dirt. She finished with her customers and we went into my office."Why havn't I screened this Jaden girl?" Momma asked sitting on the small couch in front of my desk and crossed her legs. Momma was *too* feminine. "She's very pretty Octavious, but I want to see what's on her mind. You're a helluva asset now baby, with your growing business and all. I just don't want no more drama with you son. I did four years, day for day *with* you!" She looked at her Rolex I had bought her five years ago.

"I know, thank you momma." I said opening my lap top.

"No problemo. You know what?" Momma asked. "Nu unh, I don't think I've met him before!" I said and momma smirked and rolled her eyes.

"I think you and Tiff..." "Momma, if it ain't you, it's Me-Me. How much Tiff paying yall?" I cut her off and she gave me a surrender gesture. Me-Me walked in, sat on the couch beside momma and mimicked her.

"Momma, can I go to the baby shower with you and Latunda?" Malicia asked momma. I was about to ask her something but she answered before I could. "I didn't ask you daddy cause this is girly stuff and your a *very* busy man!"

I smirked.

She smiled. They went off into their own world as I went to my T.G. VIP Club database to check the schedule. I was throwing two parties on Me-Me's birthday. One for her and one for Trapstah. But today, I had a photo shoot with a Ms.Maria Cruz.

————))(()((————

It had been a while since I had seen her from the first encounter at the Pizzeria. Today this Latino honey with hair damn near to her ass was looking like a piece of butterscotch candy, mouthwatering.

We had talked a few times and had learned a great deal together about photography and venturing in it as a business. She was currently running a nail salon. Over all, she was a bad bitch. We met up two hours before the shoot at Chili's in Little Rock.

"I think this here is going to be big." I said while nibling a Cajun fry. I was across from her at our table and she shared the fries with me while we sipped wine.

"Yeah, I think so too." Maria said eating as femine as you could possibly think. She had a strong Spanish accent with perfect white teeth like Tiffany, but had one of those sexy over bites like Lauren London."These fries are *too* good!" Maria smiled at me. "So your girlfriend is your assistant and business manager?" "Yeah.She's good people, and her business mind is sharp." I said with eye contact.

————))(()((————

"That's good news, let's do this!" She smiled again and we shook on it.

The first shoot was one I stole from Buffy The Body. Maria had on a bikini top with a pair of perfect fitting Apple Bottoms and Stillettos.

"Your hair is the shit!" I said as Jaden worked with her make up to fit the lighting. "Thanks!" Maria said body glistening and glowing. I instantly imagined me hitting it from the back.

"You have nice hips!" Jaden complimented. She was eyeing Maria's body nonchalantly. "They fit your frame perfectly!"

"Thanks!" Maria smiled at Jaden. "Why am I nervous?"

"Natural instinct, being that you are a sexy person!" I complimented and she blushed. "who's your favorite singer?"

"Right now, J.Holiday!" Maria said getting comfortable as Jaden finished her hair. I surfed the net on my lap top and filled the air with J. Holiday's "Bed."

"Ooh, that's my song!" Maria said real feminine and cute.

The photo shoot turned out to be a succes. We went from a motorcycle shoot, to a beach, to a mansion in southwest Little Rock. I had Maria in the skimpiest school Teacher outfit ever and her body was honey roasted with perfect curves.

"That's it baby! Do your thang girl, looking good!" I encouraged as Maria constantly posed and modeled at me through the camera. "Say I'm sexy!" I encouraged.

"I'm sexy baby!" she responded giving me her all. I knew I had got all good shots from the start cause my dick was leaking. I was ready to fuck this spanish piece of candy.

"Ooh girl! You're workin it!" That was Jaden. She was always the perfect assistant. She's a plus at helping me keeping the models alive in these shoots. Jaden had told me that she went both ways but the dick was good enough for her right now. "Girl, you got it hot up in here!" Jaden beamed at her causing Maria to become so comfortable that she blushed.

Jaden caught it and took advantage, and kissed the side of her mouth. Maria smiled unbelievably and looked at me. I snapped the best picture of the whole shoot.

We went to dinner at Garfield's and I had the two baddest

feminine creatures in the building. Jaden was Prada down and Maria Baby Phat. Both in Stilletos. The food hadn't blown my high, and I was talking about *everybody* in the restaurant. "Look at this ma fucka here!" I spoke in a whisper and pointed with my eyes at this wanna be thug with a Boosie fade, with a hundred thousand worth of fake jewelry. "This nigga got his Ice out the back of a Source magazine!" We laughed under our breath.

"Shit ain't even shining!" Jaden giggled."

"Is that a paper clip holding it together?" That was Maria. She had the prettiest little mouth.

"Ay, let's get out of here, go shoot some pool or something?" I suggested.

"No! Let's go cut a few rugs!" Jaden recommended.

"Yes!" Maria agreed.

———⸺◉⸺———

I was driving a rented Dodge Ram Truck with Maria in the middle and Jaden the passenger seat. The wine had the girls tipsy as we made stimulating conversation.

"Personally, I think that women are able to run a country but right now, they need some nuts up in there!" I said of our political debate. "I think that you're absolutely right because there's a lot of other agendas going on that, the media's not allowed to publicize." Jaden said. She could make you sometimes forget that she was a dangerous gangsta bitch.

"You ain't never lying!" Maria concurred.

"I do admit that women in Politics know how to play their position." I said stopping at a light. "That's in *every* position!" Jaden said with her beautiful self.

"Claro Que si!" Maria said seductively. "What doea that mean?" I asked looking in her eyes. "For sure!" Maria said looking at me, then at Jaden, then at her pretty little hands in her lap. "Where's your man?" Jaden asked with a side glance. "Beautiful as you are I know you have one."

"Nope. I'm loving the single life! Allows me to give my career my all." Maria said.

"Ever tasted the rainbow?" Jaden asked and looked at me then her. "And I think he's a virgin in the voyerism if it." Jaden purred at Maria and kissed her ear. She had just told her that she wanted me to watch them get down. I don't think I could have been as smooth. Jaden twisted in her seat and faced me and Maria's sideview."I know you digging my man Maria. I know he's feeling you too. Your a beautiful girl!" Jaden rubbed Maria cheek. "I'm ma be straight up, the only way your fucking him is with me present, and I'm participating, ain't that right baby?" Jaden asked me while eyeing Maria and placing some loose hair behind her ear. "Already!" I said giving Maria a look over.

"Ya'll are a hot mess!" Maria said placing a hand on Jaden's thick thigh. Jaden planted a soft kiss on her lips.

"All mothafuckin ready!" I said pulling off at the light.

Chapter 14
"OG"

We went to a club in Fayetteville to get our dance on. The club was on fire as Jeezy and R. Kelly let us know they were "Go Gettas." We posted up at the bar and ordered six shots of Patron and Apple Martinis.

"Damn shawty, you's a female pimp ain't you?" I said cooly to Jaden. Maria smirked.

"All the time!" Jaden bragged.

"You know pimps can get pimped too!" Maria said with a sexy side glance. "Any how!" I said as if they wasn't talking about nothing." "I thought yall wanted to dance with a nigga?" Justin Timberlake's "Until The End of Time" blared out and they dragged me out on the dance floor and malested me. Maria was holding me from the front grinding her five foot five frame against me. Jaden was behind me rubbing her hands up and down my six pack.

"You want to fuck her don't you?" She said in my ear then stuck her tongue in it.

"You?" I answered with a question.

"If you want me to!" Jaden offered and massaged my erection. Jaden then placed Maria hands on it and from her expression I could tell she was a size Queen.

"I see that you *are* as Tall as you are Tall!" Maria said in my ear and I heard some smacking. Her and Jaden had started kissing. My dick threatened to bust out of my Evisu Jeans. Jaden had a bottle of Cristal and gave Maria a swallow. She then kissed me and gave me an Ex pill with her mouth. I chewed it up and took a swig of champagne.

"Let's go get on some gangsta shit!" I said to the girls.

We went to Oil Can's apartment and found a bag of Ex pills of all sorts. We chewed another Ex and popped some more bottles of champagne. I snatched my shirt off and swung my chain cause I just *knew* Maria would have some good pussy.

"What you smiling at?" Maria inquired after catching me gawking at her fat ass booty.

"I'm ready to make you scream a nigga name out!" I said going into the kitchen to roll up a blunt. "Me too!" Jaden said to Maria and led her in the kitchen with me. "Kiss her baby!" Jaden said to me, slowly caressing Maria's C cups. I done as told and got deep in our kiss. The next thing I knew we were completely naked. I put some fire to the blunt as Maria kissed on the Trapstah house that was on my chest.

"Taste daddy's dick!" Jaden instructed as Maria went down on me. She had some nice orals as Jaden got some ice out the freezer and sucked on my chest with some in her mouth. She went down and helped Maria. They took turns sucking, slurping, gobbling, and deep throating my dick and balls.

"It taste so delicious and juicy!" Maria said between slurps. The Extacy made the freak come running out her like Micheal Vick.

"Suck that dick girl! Do yo thang! Ya'll kiss on it!" I directed as they kissed and pecked my dick. Then each other. I pulled Maria up and stood her against the fridge. Jaden fed her a strawberry as I went down and threw one of Maria legs over my shoulder. I sucked and licked her clit while Jaden sucked her collar bone. "Oh my God! I'm cuming... shit I'm cuming!" Maria moaned in a deep sweat. Her pussy tasted good and I applied pressure on her clit and she came in my mouth. I came up, spinned Jaden around and started sucking on her back as she arched it.

Maria played with Jaden's nipples. I got so freaky that I ran my tongue down between her ass and licked it. I spreaded her cheeks and licked her ass clean.

"Ahh shit!... Stop! Stop! Stop!... Baby it feel too good!" Jaden screamed and squirmed. "Make her feel it! Make her cum daddy!" Maria encouraged and Jaden came and had juices running down her thighs. I went into the bedroom, grabbed a hand full of rubbers, and went back to find Jaden sucking the hell out of Maria's pussy. Maria was on her back so i stood over them and masterbated. They both got turned on by my pervertedness.

"Let up baby, let me punch on that pussy!" I said to Jaden as I eased inside her from the back as she continued to eat up Maria. I made the dick good to where she couldn't concentrate.

"Ooh OG baby! You in my stomach! Your dick feel so good!" Jaden moaned, squeezing on Maria's titties. I started punching in and out vigorously and felt her cum and start trembling.

I then gave her three more back to back.

I now had Maria on the counter sliding my dick up and down between her love folds. She grabbed it and guided it in her. I long stroked her real hard while Jaden sucked my neck from behind me. "Fuck her daddy! Give her *all* that big dick! Make her come for me OG!" Jaden said pushing on my hips as Maria worked up an orgasim. "I'm cuming!...I'm cuming!.. God!" She moaned and grinded back at me.

"Tell me that dick good shawty! Now!" I said snatching her off the counter while bouncing her on my dick. I gripped her ass and made her catch my rythym.

"Your dick is good!...Aahh!...Shit! Oh my God! Hold up!..Aah!" Maria yelled and creamed all over me. I sat her down and she caught a shiver and glowed. "Wow! Who knew dick could be so good!" Maria said fanning herself.

"Dope dick!" That was Jaden. The Ex pills had us dripping sweat. She was looking at my still hard dick as I stood with my legs open relighting the blunt that had went out. I swigged champagne, burped and looked at them catching their breath. From the look of my dick they knew they was in for a long night. Literally.

———— ⋙«◉»⋘ ————

Jaden and I was inseperable the rest of the week. She was so easy to make conversation with. We worked with Maria's shoot and put together a web page. I recorded each photo shoot and interviewed each model to create them a nice blog. I took some naked pictures of Jaden and sent them to the big homies along with some money orders. They would be jacking off to Jaden's fine ass for a long time. We were still posted at Oil Can's apartment as Oil came and went. We both had our lap tops as our company as we mingled and worked. Jaden knew exactly how much space to give a man at the right times. She seemed to have a beautiful spirit and could very well be wifey material.

If I didn't know any better.

I was running an investigation on her ass which led me to find out that she had a child. I still had sources all over the state of Arkansas. If she'll lie about simple shit, then she must be hiding something. The day I found out about her child I took us to get tested. For *everything*. We both came up clean as a whistle.

It was a few hours before Me-Me's first party and I finally closed my lap top. Jaden came from the kitchen in a Vicky Secret teddie. She had made me breakfast. Kiesha Cole was blowing in the back somewhere as Jaden sat in my lap. Her fresh-out-the-shower scent was intoxicating.

"You okay? You got five hours in staight!" Jaden said looking in my eyes. She kissed the side of my mouth. "Why you always kiss the side of peoples' mouth?"

"That's where all the flavor is at!" She said puckering her glossed lips wanting a peck. I kissed the side of her mouth and she giggled. I rubbed her love muscle and she gently jumped.

"Ooh un unh. You been fucking me to *death* these last couple of days and my stuff is sore!" Jaden said grabbing my hand and played with my fingers. "We got to take a couple days off!"

"I beats it up like that?" My ego asked.

"Man!" Jaden fanned her self and acted as if she needed some air. "My pussy be crying and *begging* for mercy!"

"N-E-way!" I said with ego satisfied."Gone and get ready shaw-ty. Roll up a few blunts and get me something fresh out." I said as she got up.

"Already!" Jaden smiled and I palmed her phat booty. I watched her feminine swagger as she went into the bedroom. I loved the way her ass swayed from left to right on top of her bowed legs. Too bad that all this would have to end when Tiffany decides that she wants us to be together. Tiff and momma was the *only* two women I trusted. In the year we messed around before I went to prison, we had went through *ten* years of drama.I cheated on the regular and she kept her promise of allowing me to be Malicia's father, rather she had a man or not. So if she made the decision now of us being together, I would drop Jaden without thinking about it. But in the mean time, Jaden was my bottom bitch. She was smart, sexually de-fiant, pretty with a banging body, and as gangsta as they come. I had a big surprise for her at the second party. I was about to change the game in the Bluff.

Malicia's official party was at Big Banjo Pizza Palace back in Pine Bluff. I went straight to the shop and got the Purple H3 with "T.G. Detail" in the paint. A rolling commercial. Oil Can put ten grand worth of entertainment in it and the back was filled with gifts for Me-Me. We pulled up ten minutes early with the system pumping *Shawty Lo* through the four twelve inch kickers. Jaden and I both were rocking Gucci fits. My only diamonds were in my ears. We walked into the party and Malicia was waiting in front of the doors with her hands on her hips.

"I said to be here thirty minutes early! Geesh!" Malicia said rocking on one of her little hips and crossing her arms. "My bad. I stopped to get gas." I lied.

"The hummer was full. Your lying daddy, and this must be Jaden!" Malicia smiled at her.

"Yes I'm Jaden! As beautiful as you are, you are most definitely Me-Me!" Jaden beamed. Malicia beamed back.

"Good. Don't ever have him this late!" Malicia gave a stern look. "The party has started, yall come on!" Malicia said grabbed each of our hands and led us to the party.

I caught it the instant I seen her look at us.

Tiffany did not like what she was seeing as Me-Me led us by hand up to her and Neko.

"What it is my nigga?" I asked Neko and gave him some dap.

"Maintainin."Neko said with Tiffany in his lap.

"What's up shawty?" He spoke to Jaden. "I'm good! How you doing Tiffany?" Jaden smiled at her.

"I'm good!" Tiffany smiled back. "Hey OG, Me-Me was about to have a fit!"

"Sure was!" That was Malicia." You let uncle Javon beat you

here!" She said referring to Oil Can by his Government. Oil Can and Limira were talking to momma and Oil Can's momma.

"I like the Hummer!" Tiffany said.

"Yeah that's just advetisement for the shop." I said and sat down and I put Jaden hands on my shoulder for a massage.

"What ya'll got up?" I asked Tiffany.

"Not shit! Get this party out the way and go home and get some rest!" Tiffany said rubbing Neko's head like she used to do me. She was doing it just to fuck with me. Just like I was doing with the massage.

"Fa real?" I asked.

"Yes! I *been* tired of school and the organization is time consuming. I need a good night sleep!" Tiffany said. She looked at me and dropped her head real smooth. I could tell that she didn't want Jaden here.

"I know how you feel girl!" Jaden said then beamed at Neko who seemed to be hypnotized by her glamour. I prayed that Tiffany didn't catch it. "OG and I barely see each other and it seems as if I'm always working!"

"Exactly!" Tiffany concurred. She smiled at Jaden. "Finally, someone who knows *exactly*!" "Well I think I have the hardest job of all!" I said.

"And that is?" Tiffany asked.

"I'm trying to get Trapper of the year. I'm a Trapstah Gangsta and *I say* we move corperate with our trapping. I'mma take the dope out the hood and sell it in society. You know what the highest and easiest selling drug in America is? I asked looking at Neko.

"What it is my nigga?" He asked rubbing Tiff's leg. "Sex. Sex is selling like cell phones! And I got a plan!" I said and kissed Jaden's hand and pulled her in my lap where she fitted comfortably. Malicia covered her ears and ran off.

"What you got up homie?" Neko curiously asked. "I'm about to get on some Internet shit with this white boy. I think it's gonna be big?" I said and watched Tiffany through my peripheral as I rubbed Jaden's exposed calves. Jaden had Gymnest legs that were seductively bowed like Halle Berry. I could see Tiffany mentally roll her eyes. Oil Can and Lamira broke our secret agrivation.

"Man, ya'll can get the fuck out my apartment cause I'm coming home tonight. Lamira's gone hold that down anyway." Oil Can said holding Lamira from behind. Oil has never had a girlfriend over a year. It was no surprise that Lamira would eventually move in. And it won't be over six months from now that someone else will replace her.

"Man shut up!" I said and thumped his head and we did our shake. "Appreciate the Hummer brah. Guess what nigga?"

"What it is?" Oil Can asked, mouth sparkling.

"I got an idea! I'mma tell you later!" I said and Tiffany, Jaden, and Lamira all smacked their lips in unison. "N-T-Way!" Tiffany said and rolled her eyes.

"Fa real!" Jaden said and did her eye roll.

"Already!" Lamira was the closer with hers. And each nigga gave their girl a look to say *mind your business*!

Malicia's first party was a success and I admit, I did over do it with the gifts. Oil Can didn't make it no better showering her with multicolored diamonds that him and Lamira went and got in Houston, Texas. She had more clothes that she would grow out of before she would get a chance to wear. She wasn't allowed to have any more toys. She already had *too* many. Her and momma acted a plum fool on stage and had a good time. everybody mingled for a few minutes while Oil jumped on the phone. I agreed to meet with my daughter for a session of CNN tomorrow and left for her second party that she was not attending. Momma and Tiffany tried to come but got shot down before Quick got ready.

We were gliding down University in the Hummer bumping the Pimpalation DVD, watching Pimp C talk a gang of shit. I loved UGK to death. Lamira and Oil Can was in the back making small talk. I kept seeing her watching me in the rearview mirror. I wanted to melt that bar of chocolate with my mouth and let it run down the sides. I looked at Jaden who was watching me watch her and winked her eye at me then went back to the movie. We had club *Twenty Four* on lock for the next couple of hours. There was at least four girls to every Trapstah. I had the cameras rolling already when we pulled up to the front bumping Lil Wayne and Baby's *"Leather So Soft"* and shook the ground. This was me and Oil's moment cause we were the stars of this party. Every girl in the building would wish they were in Jaden and Lamira shoes. Cool and Pimp had a group of girls strapped up with pistols as we made our way through the club. It seems as if we were strolling in slow motion as the Trapstah anthem kicked in. Young Jeezy's *Trap or Die* had me walking with a helluva swagger. We made it to our VIP section and posted up. We had a view of the club and it was Trapstahs, people invited, and enough women for orgies. We started popping bottles and passing blunts. Jaden got loose and started grinding against me. I was behind her with my arms around her waist.

"Man, I'm feeling myself!" Jaden said. Her perfume was intoxicating.

"Yeah? And why is that?"

"Cause I'm getting money, and got a *real* nigga on my team!" She said sounding sincere.

"You my Bonnie?" I asked and bit her ear. "You my *Clyde*?" Jaden answered with a question. "Already!"

"That's what's up!" Jaden affirmed and looked up sideways for a peck on the lips. "Look at all these hoes watching me, wanting you!" She giggled.

"Like you say, because I'm the realest nigga in the building. I *better* have the realest bitch in the building!"

"Already!" Jaden said grabbing my fingers. Lamira brought up a bottle of Crissy.

"I need for you to handle something for me then." I said rubbing across her flat stomach. "You see that nigga over their dancing with the girl in the white Baby Phat outfit?" Jaden only took a second to spot him.

"Yeah with the stunna shades and the chain with the platinum chicken?" She had him.

"Yeah, the nigga is working with the Alphabet boys. FBI, I invited him to alliviate that problem. Bring me that nigga chain."

I knew the only way you could get the nigga named Chicken Hawk's chain was to kill or be killed. The nigga might have been snitching but that don't mean he won't kill you, and he was known for it.

"Already." Jaden said as if she was already formatting a plan to handle it. She kissed me then eased off to Lamira and they crept off. I went and sat with Oil Can and Pimp on the couch. Cool was in a chair with a Chinese doll.

"Look at this nigga Cool!" I said hitting Oil Can on the arm. "Nigga that's a bad bitch!"

"Nigga the whole club is full of bad hoes!" Oil Can said and did a line of powder. I used to love it just as much as him, but prison took the habit. "Nigga I got to sweat this drop tomorrow. How much of that shit is now clean?" Oil Can asked of our money.

"One hundred fifty thousand, eight hundred and two dollars."

"Already!" Oil Can said and rubbed his face. "That nigga Tay shot two Loot dogs a few minutes ago. Nigga, that's ten of them niggas we done hit. I reallly want to bring it to them niggas but we doing our thang. So fuck it, play chess with the niggas for a minute."

"Already." I said trusting his art of war. "I also got a feeling them Eastside niggas is lurkin, but I'm on it. I might as well get rid of them niggas so I don't have to worry about them niggas getting me." "Already. Put it together and fill me in brah." Oil Can said and did another line. I sipped my champagne and thought about what I had just said. Them niggas was out to get me. I could feel it. So it was kill or be killed.

And if Jaden handles her business with Chicken Hawk, then she may become First Lady of the click.

Chapter 15
"Jaden"

I seductively walked up on the man with the iced out chicken doing his two step. "Damn!" What it is shawty?" Chicken chain asked me with lust in his ugly ass eyes. Big and open like a crackhead, looking animated in his shades.

"You!" I said standing back on my bow legs and making my ass slightly bounce. "Can I holla?" "Already! Come on shawty, let's mob the bar. I'm that nigga Chicken Hawk. Who you?"

"I'm Lisa!" I seductively stared into his eyes as we strolled towards the bar. I had Lamira on her way to get a room under one of her many fake ID's. I had a plan.

"What you drankin shawty?" Chicken Hawk asked with a mouth full of diamonds.

"My favorite, Pina Colada!" I lied. Just as I did with OG with the Apple Martini. "I like your grill, and you are *so* thug! I'm feeling you! I think you real!" I rubbed his face. He moved my hand from his face.

"Hold up shawty, you moving fast like you rolling on Extacy!" Chicken Hawk said and ordered some Pa'tron.

"Nigga I'm just a gangster bitch! I'm for real with it!" I said with a sexy screw face. Chicken Hawk smiled and his nose got wide.

"Already shawty! I appologize for asassinating your character!" He said and downed two of his six shots. I downed one of them.

"This is a live party and all but I'm ready to go. What it is with you?" I asked with massive sex appeal.

"I'm here with my niggas." Chicken Hawk said and got in my face. "You a bad mothafucka! You know that?" He observed the crowd to see if anybody was watching him. "My girlfriend tells me that all the time!" I said to where he could smell my breath. "We got a room, and I'm ready to go!"

—————————————

Lamira was popping a bottle of champagne when we stepped into our room at the Best Western. She had texted me the location and room number while we was leaving the parking lot of the club.

"Hey baby!" I said to Lamira and gave her a peck. "Look what I caught!"

Lamira had on a Prada body suit the same color her skin, looking like an appetizer.

"You caught the biggest fish in the sea!" Lamira boosted Chicken Hawk's ego while eyeing the chain that was about to cost him his life.

"Damn! ya'll is what's up!" Chicken Hawk smiled a glittery smile and eased up on me from behind and put his dick on my ass.

"No, nigga, you is what's up!" I said grinding against him when Lamira turned the TV to videos. His dick was hard instantly. "Ooh, nigga you packing a magnum ain't you!" I complemented his dick size factitously. It was barely poking, and *then* he was ugly. Lamira swigged her champagne and came upon us and stuck her tongue in my mouth. We allowed it to get good and we had Chicken man hypnotized. We broke our kiss. "You like that big boy!" I said and kissed the side of his mouth. That was the signal for Lamira to say she was about to roll a blunt and go put some Visene on her titties.

"Ooh, let me roll some weed!" She played her position.

"What's her name?" Chicken Hawk asked.

"Mary." I said.

"I'm about to blow up, ya'll wanna be in my video?" Chicken Hawk asked.

"Already!" I pecked him again.

Lamira fired up the blunt and by the time we made it half way through it, while talking all nasty, I all of a sudden grabbed Chicken Hawk's nub of a dick and massaged it through his pants.

"I want the dick first!" I said to Lamira and she pulled her titties out and put them in Chicken Hawk's face.

"Nu unh! I'm first! Huh nigga, suck these!" She placed a pretty C cup in his mouth and he sucked away. Nigga get naked!" I demanded as Lamira and I slowly got undressed. I popped back on my legs and Chicken Hawk's little dick was leaking. I had to give the Visene time to kick in. He was finally naked with that stupid looking chicken chain around his neck. I started dancing with Lamira as she kissed my collar bone and neck; I damn near got horny for real. We eased up on Chicken Hawk as he began to feel the Visene he'd sucked off Lamira breast.

"Tonight's your night big daddy!" I said and kissed his neck as Lamira eased off to wipe down the room with bleach. "You taste like a man that knows how to fuck!" I said with another kiss to his neck and gently flipped the razor from under my tongue. I gripped it between my teeth and sliced him from ear to ear in one motion. I had the razor back under my tongue before I could look back at him and before he knew he was cut. "To bad it was you who got fucked!" I smirked at him. I stepped back cause I knew he would try to speak and would shoot blood everywhere. The weed, liquor, and visene created a panic in him and he started grasping for air. Everytime he tried to speak he made a gargling noise with squrits of blood. He stumbled then down to the floor, back grabbing at his neck and fell against the bed. His eyes were beach balls as I left him dying to help

Lamira wipe things down. I put on some Latex gloves and took the chain off Chicken Hawk's dead body. I sprayed alcohol on his neck and wiped off my kisses.

We left and went back to the party. It had took less that an hour to handle the job and the party was just starting to jump. OG and Oil Can had some strippers drop it like it's hot to Snoop's song of the same title. Cool and Pimp was stepping like they were drunk as drunk. "Where you been at?" Oil Can asked Lamira as she wrapped him around her.

"To and fro!" Lamira said enjoying his embrace like a kitten.

"Send them hoes out of here!" I said to OG while sitting in his lap. "Lamira and I can do better than that! Matter of fact, Hey! Ya'll can leave now!" I said to the two big booty strippers that was mouth watering. I wanted to taste the chocolate one's sweat that was drizzling down the side of her face. I got up and got in her face. "You're the sexeist bitch I've seen thus far!" I said seductively and ran my pinky nail down her topless chest and across her nipple. She flushed over and blushed with embarresment."I'll get to you later. Don't leave yet." I said to her ass. Her friend smiled at me. "We'll holla at you!" I said giving her her dismissal. "OG, baby come here!" I said as he eased up behind me. "Look at her baby! Ain't she a doll?" I asked him rubbing my hands up and down his arms and fitting up against him.

"Yeah, she thick as fuck!" OG said into my ear.

"You wanna fuck her?"

"You?" "Nah, but I want to watch you fuck her!" I said. I wanted to see someone take the fucking that he put on my ass, and *then* he had a big dick.

"Whatever pleases you baby!" OG said and squeezed me.

OG tore stripper girl's ass to pieces. Bad enough she couldn't take no dick, but she got placd in positions she never thought existed. She moaned and screamed and tried to run but to no avail. She received the fucking of her life. We had a room on the Westside and stripper girl, also known as Delight, had overdicked and was snoring in a fetal position.

"Where did you go earlier?" OG asked with his lap top in his lap. He was still naked. I gazed at his weapon that looked dangerous on standby.

"To get you a surprise!" I said standing in front of him with some girly short shorts and a Baby Phat tank top. I had a bottle of Crissy and had popped an Extacy pill. I walked up on him and placed one in his mouth and left for the batheroom. I pulled Chicken Hawks chain out of my duffle bag. I had the chain in a ziplock bag with Chicken Hawk's blood still on it. I walked back up on OG with it behind my back. When he looked up I held it out to him.

"That's my girl!" OG said with a sunny day smile while motioning for me to sit in his lap. I did as suggested.

"Nigga I'm your Bonnie!" I looked at him all girly.

"That's what's up!" OG said and kissed me. "I'm yo Clyde!"

"Fa real?"

"Fa real!"

"Well, this is what it is." I began before the Extacy pill really took affect. "I need a favor too!"

"Fa real?" OG asked giving life to a blunt. "Fa real. But I'll let you know when. Right now, I want some dick. You know I recorded you and stripper girl!"

"That's why you was all in a nigga face with that thang?" OG asked referring to my camcorder. "Yep!" I said feeling the Ex pill. I pulled two more out of the ziplock bag full on the table. We both chewed one. "I'mma make her a contract that sells her out at five hundred dollars."

"Hell, in that case, put her in your stable you're about to establish through Trapstah." OG said seriously. Good. I *got* him. Now I got the advantage of taxing the Eastside Pirus and then play both sides and let them kill each other.

"Already!" I said anticipating the good fucking I was about to recieve.

———»《◎》«———

"He just told me *that* last week." I informed Popcorn and Demon. Two days had past and Lamira and I were reporting to the Eastside Pirus our latest accomplishments.

"Them niggas ain't playing! They getting money! And then they cleaning it up quick through all types of organizations." Lamira said to make them envious with hate. And then I dropped the bomb.

"And *then* they braggin about killing your brotha. How they caught him in the club and pumped a whole clip in him." I said playing with Popcorn and Demon's emotions. Popcorn jumped up, grabbed me around my neck, and pinned me against the wall. I was off my feet before *Quick* got *ready*.

"Hold up, nigga!" Lamira said with her P90 pistol to the side of Popcorn's head. "You need to calm the fuck down! That's Jaden, not that nigga OG! We're doing as told nigga! To report *everything*! Now, get your mothafuckin hands off her!" She put her gun back in her clutch.

"Ya'll bitchs is crazy." Demon said nonchalant reading a novel called *One Eleven*. Popcorn released me and I didn't lose my woman hood.

"Look. I got the nigga OG just as Lamira got Oil Can. First, we learn them niggas. Oil Can is handling the click and the connects while OG cleans it up. Be patient with us and let us do our thing." I looked Popcorn in the eye. "How bad you want this nigga?"

"Bad." Popcorn said with watery eyes.

"Twenty five a piece for right now. I *promise* you it will be worth it." I said.

"Pussy is a mothafucka!" Demon said as he turned a page in his novel.

"Nawl nigga, it ain't the pussy." Lamira said seductively twisting her hair. "It's knowing how to play your position. It don't get no gangsta than that!"

"Amen!" I cosigned.

"I tell ya'll what, let's go get a bite to eat!" Demon smiled for the first time in his life, which made him even uglier.

We left Pine Bluff and headed to Dumas in Popcorn's big body Benz. Woodgrain was everywhere creating a perfect match with the soft leather.

"You miss a nigga don't you Lamira?" Popcorn asked driving like an old man. Lamira was on the passenger side with me behind her. Demon was beside me looking as ugly as ever.

"Miss that dick of yours!" Lamira mumbled real sexy. She could have made the cover of the Biggest Liar Ever magazine with that one. She told me how his dick impersonated the Planter's Peanut when he was on hard.

"You miss that dick huh?" Popcorn's ego was blushing. He put some hair behind Lamira's ear and rubbed her jaw. "I got that dope dick!"

"Sure do!" Lamira made the cover again.

"Miss Jaden," Demon started while looking in my eyes, "you mind if we made conversation?" He asked.

"Sure, what it is?" I asked since he was nice about it.

"Well, I know you be thinking that I'm the ugliest nigga that you've seen thus far, but I tell you I'mma cool nigga with a helluva swagger. Get past the looks and see the potential." Demon said and his ugly ass made me blush. That shit was gangsta!

"We'll see." I smiled at him and he all of a sudden became an ugly cute with his muscled up arms and chest in his tank top.

We made it to Dumas and copped a back table at McDonald's. The purple weed we had smoked had us wanting to eat up everything. We then discussed everything there was of Oil Can and OG and then decided to go on to Mississippi to the casino.

Our room at the casino was plush with a balcony overlooking the Mississippi River. Lamira throwed up for no reason at all. The first thing that came to mind was that she's pregnant but I knew she wouldn't play herself like that. My Aisa had come from a one night stand and I couldn't stand her dead beat dad.

"Stomach virus?" I asked when she came out the bathroom from freshening up.

"Or *something*!" Lamira said with a cute frown and plopped down beside me. I rolled a blunt and shared a bottle of champagne with Lamira. Popcorn and Demon sat across from us looking at us like they were crazy.

"What the hell?" I asked of their looks.

"Fa real!" Lamira had my back as she seductively hit the blunt. I sipped the champagne from the bottle through a straw.

"Ya'll *know* what it is?" Popcorn said hitting a line of cocaine and chewing an Extacy pill. Demon was looking at me with a persona when he did his line. "Nigga it is what it is!" I said and accepted a charge from the blunt from Lamira. "Let me see what you working with!" I said and threw my legs across Lamira's lap. She slowly stroked them. Popcorn got naked before *Quick* got *ready*. I looked at his little hard dick, and then it had the nerves to be crooked. "Yo turn nigga!" I said to Demon to keep from laughing at Popcorn's nugget.

I pulled Lamira's face to mine and we started kissing. She eased on top of me and we started grinding against each other. It got good and I pulled her top down and licked her nipples.

"Damn!" Lamira all of a sudden said looking at Demon. I followed her eyes to see the biggest dick I had ever seen in my life! This nigga had at least twelve inches that was *too* thick, and then he wasn't hard. "Nigga, you need to be arrested for having a dick that big!" I said knowing good and *damn* well I couldn't fuck with him. Popcorn seemed to be envious of his package but still held his ground and stroked his Hershey minature. Lamira eased a finger in me and stimulated my clitorus and I came instantly and went down on her. Her pussy tasted so good to my taste buds. Popcorn and Demon were in awe as Lamira came all over my pretty face.

I looked at Demon's now hard dick which was looking like the Statue of Liberty. They both started reaching in their pants on the floor and pulled out stacks of money and cheering us on.

"Do that shit girl! Do that shit!" Popcorn cheered peeling of twenties and making them rain down on us as I brought Lamira to her second one.

"All mothafuckin ready!" Demon said being just as friendly with his money. "That's what's up!" He was stroking his monster and as bad as I wanted to go for a test drive I couldn't build the nerve. His dick was the first I actually feared. Lamira had me screaming as she gave me three back to back. We were damn near covered in money. Demon walked up on me and put his dick in my face while I laid there on my back with Lamira giving me my tongue lashing. Me being the freak I am, I grabbed it and kissed it.

"Damn!" I said of it's thickness. I tried to suck it and couldn't get the head of it in my mouth. So I licked it and kissed it while he stroked it."Cum on my titties!"

This nigga shot enough cum to fill up a foot tub. There was enough to bring about a tribe.

"Ahh shit! Damn!...Damn you got some pretty titties!" Demon said as he came, rubbing his semen across my nipples, causing some of the money to stick.

We cleaned up, went shopping with the four thousand a piece that Lamira and I had earned without intint, and went to a Yo Gotti concert. Popcorn and Demon had us backstage without passes and we mingled with the rappers and ballers. We entered someone's dressing room and everybody showed Demon and Popcorn love. I smelled weed.

"What it is shawty?" Some guy asked with diamonds everywhere.

"Nothin!" I said all shy and cute. "I'm Jaden and this my BFF Lamira."

"Hey!" Lamira said like a model, but being a diva.

"I'm that nigga Webbie."

"We know who you are! Nigga duh!" I lied but knew the name."Where's Boosie!"

"Ah shit! Boosie!...Boosie come here nigga!" Webbie yelled as a dark skin dude made his way over. He looked young and full of energy.

"Hey Boosie!" I said hoping that he was him.

"Hey gurl! Don't I know you from somewhere?" Boosie asked, smelling like purple weed. His accent was New Orleans.

"Probably not, I would have left an impression!" I flirted and smiled."This is my girl Lamira." "Your girl?" Boosie asked.

"Yeah."

"Your *girl* girl?" That was Webbie.

"Yeah nigga, my girl *and* my girl!" I said giving them both a sexy screw face. They both looked at each other as if to say 'damn!' "That's what's up!" They said in unison. We exchanged numbers and caught up with Demon and Popcorn who were smoking a blunt with Yo Gotti. We were introduced by Demon.

"Hey Gotti!" I said like I knew him personally.

"What up shawty."He said just as cool. His grill *had* to be at least fifty thousand. We was excused and they went back to talking.

After thirty minutes of exchanging numbers we shot back to the room. I was high and tired and ready to get some z's. I was in the front of the presidental while Lamira and Popcorn was in the bedroom. Demon was naked again, not from wanting some pussy, but from popping Extacy and snorting cocaine. His dick was so big, on soft, that it didn't even turn me on.

"Do you get much pussy?" I *had* to ask.

"Hell yeah!" Demon said grinding his teeth and sweating. My braces were starting to hurt. "Fa real? Yo shit is too big for me Demon. Fa real." I said being honest. "Sorry." I added to let him know that ain't no way in the hell he was sticking that Pringle can up in me.

"I'm good. Plus I'm numb anyway." He said and started counting a duffle bag of money. My phone rung. It was OG. "Hey baby!" I chimed.

"What it is shawty?"

"Shit. Bored shopping with my Auntie...my boyfriend." I said and acted like she had asked who it was, at the same time holding a finger up to my mouth at Demon for him to be quiet.

"I miss you J." OG said and I felt it. I think I was feeling OG cause he made a good friend. He was easy to talk to. I was thinking about telling him about my daughter Asia.

"I got something to tell you baby." I said.

"Damn. I can't get a *I miss you too?*"

"I miss you too boy!" I blushed not wanting too. He had that type of affection that *made* you love him no matter how hard you tried not to.

"I want to see you. Now! Where you at?" OG asked.

"In Fayetteville." I lied.

"I'm on my way." "Fa real?" I started a cool panic. I was in another state about to sleep with the enemy. I broke a sweat.

"Yeah, it won't take...hold on" OG clicked over then hung up. I called back. "I'll call you back." OG said and hung up.

Chapter 16
"Lamira"

"Yes! Oh God yes!" I faked as Popcorn rammed his Planter Peanut in me from the back. I looked back at him and gave a sex face that said he was killing it. He lit up at my fictitious gesture and slapped my ass.

"You miss this dick don't you!" Popcorn said trying to grind. "No.I miss Oil Can's dick!" I wanted to say, but instead I said,"yes! I miss daddy dick!"

Popcorn started grinding vigorously to cause some friction but to no avail. Jaden suddenly busted up in the room.

"Lamira, we got to go. Now!" She said standing at the edge of the bed, unattentive of me and Popcorn still having sex. "This nigga OG is on his way to meet us in Fayetteville and he's not answering my calls. We can't blow this *now!*" Popcorn had stopped at the mention of OG's name and was now on his feet. His thumb size condom fell off as he stared at Jaden with anger in his eyes, then turned and went into the bathroom. We left the room and rented a car, then shot back to Arkansas. Jaden dropped me off at Oil Can's and I went in and threw up again. I already knew what time it was.

I was preganant.

Even though I didn't want to be, I had to accept it. I was scared to tell Jaden becasuse I knew better. I was suppose to have had the shot but they make your ass eat up *everything*. Oil Can wasn't home which was good. When Honey had gotten the boot I was her replacement. We went and took Aids tests and had been going at it with no condoms ever since. I cleaned the house to Oil Can's standards, which was spotless, and went got some pregnacy tests. After the third opinion, I sat on the side of the bath tub wandering what was next. I couldn't believe I was pregnant by this nigga. How could I have been so stupid? I tried to call Jaden but all I could do was stare at my cell phone. I was stuck on the picture of me and Oil Can that was placed as it's wallpaper. I was really starting to feel him. I couldn't help it. His presence was so strong and thuggish but yet he could be so gentle. He made me feel like a kitten. I finally dialed jaden.

"What?" Jaden asked with a gasp.

"I'm pregnant!" I said with tears and a sniffle. I knew I had a tongue lashing coming along with the comfort I was anticipating.

"You stupid bich!

"What were you thinking?"

"I dunno Jaden, I dunno!" I cried.

"Fuck all that crying, that is *not* gonna help. You know good and damn well, we suppose to be getting these niggas connect. You *do* remember that bitch in Popcorn's crib?" Jaden asked reminding me of ole girl that had got murked for playing around. "Yeah, I *thought* yo ass would remember!"

"Jaden, I got to kill it! I can't have his baby! I just *can't!*" I said wanting her to baby me.

"*Fa real.* Hold on, I'm in here!" She yelled out. The guys just made it in, and bitch, we were in Fayetteville with Aunt Clara!" Jaden whispered what I already knew. "Who is that, is that Lamira?" I heard Oil Can say in the background. "Tell her to get her ass here! Now!"

I was about as nervous as a virgin in a Snoop Dogg Porno. I got myself together and threw on a Louis Vutton outfit with sandals to match. I downed a Red Bull and hopped in the new H3 Hummer that I literally had to climb in. This bad boy was on some gigantic ass rims and the interior matched my outfit. OG told us to always wear Loui when were driving his Advertisement cause we were the models. I headed up Olive Street thinking of all the scenarios that could playout when I made it to OG's place. To be honest, I don't want to kill no baby. That ain't right. Plus, I *do* want a child, and this nigga is my prototype. But I couldn't live with killing my baby's daddy.

Damn. I really hate myself right now.

I made it to the apartment and parked. I could hear someone arguing as I made it to the door, which was now staring at me. The door was snatched open and OG laughed and looked at me like I was crazy.

"Fuck wrong with you?" OG asked and pulled me in the apartment. "Standing there looking crazy!" He shut the door and I noticed Jaden and Oil Can were laughing too. "N-E-Way, like I was saying, so I told that nigga he had two hours to pay me!" OG said finishing up his story. I was tripping. an hour later we were playing Dominoes. We were all high as hell and sipping Cristal, as they kicked our ass.

"Balls!" Oil Can slammed his dominoe calling out his twenty points. "A left one and a right one!"

"Crown, coke, and ice!" Jaden slammed hers real feminie calling out fifteen with blank five. "Make mine the same!" OG said calling the same amount with double blank. I was left out and played my dominoe.

"It's all good, I'm about to shoot your ass though!" I said and Oil Can knocked and it was Jaden's play.

"Dominoe!" Jaden ended the session and we got twenty out their hands. Jaden and I jumped up, turned around and went to popping our asses and then high fived. after all that we still got our asses beat.

The dominoes were now just sitting there in a played pattern and unattended. Oil Can was doing a line and talking on the phone while Jaden and OG were conversating like bestfriends. I was left alone with my thoughts as I watched Oil Can. I got to figure out how to get this connect and get myself out this situation. It seems as if the only way I can get the connect was to knock Oil Can off, put all the responsibility on OG, in which he will put more on Jaden and I. Which at least should be one step closer. Unless, they allow us to go and get the work. But that don't mean that we will be meeting the connect. Damn.

"Lamira!" Oil Can popped my arm. He had a bad habit of that shit? "What it is shawty? Where yo mind at?" He looked at me with concern. Grill glistening through the little openness of his mouth. He was a very sexy thug. "All man. So much baby. So much." I said and sat in his lap. He ran his fingers across my stomach and I jumped. "Fuck wrong with you?" Oil Can asked which caused Jaden and OG to now look at me too. His ring tone kicked in. Young Jeezy's *Trap or Die* had saved my ass. "What it is? What the.. Honey? Who the fuck is this? Bitch, I know this is you Honey! Bitch yeah I bought her a Hummer! What? Bring yo ass, she sitting on my dick right now!" Oil can said and started rubbing his hand between my legs. The fabric was making my pussy wet. "That's what's up bitch!" He sat his cell on the table. "Go get the camcorder out the Hummer!"

⋙ ⦿ ⋘

I was standing in front of the door of the Hummer with the butterfly doors still up. Oil Can had everybody come outside. My instints told me some shit was about to jump off. I turned on the camcorder and backed up to get OIl Can sitting in the driver seat. He had UGK's new Cd bumping lowly in the backgroun d. "What it is world! It's yo boy Oil Can and that nigga OG!" Oil Can said to me through the camcorder. "What up pussy niggas, real niggas, hoe niggas, trill niggas, fuck boys and all!" OG said from the passenger smoking a blunt.

"We chillin down here in the Bluff." Oil Can started. "That's Pine Bluff,Arkansas bitch! Let me tell it how it is. Now, I got this bitch about to come over here and try to whoop my bottom bitch!" Oil Can said.

"What?" I said from behind the camcorder. I just knew he was bullshitting.

"Yeah baby, this bitch Honey said she was about to kick yo ass!" Oil Can came down to me and grabbed the camcorder and was now recording me. "I told her she was a mothafuckin lie! My baby don't play no silly games!"

My heart sunk. Not because I was scared, but because I wanted to tell Oil Can I was pregnant. Plus I was fly as hell and wasn't in the mood. A white camary pulled up in the lot and and befor I knew it Honey was up in my face. Jaden was at my side from out of nowhere.

"You the bitch that cut up my clothes?" Honey mugged me with hate. This shit was happening *too* fast.

"Hold up lil momma, slow yo roll!" I said as cool as possible.

"Hold up?" Oil Can yelled at me. "Baby whoop that bitch!" Honey took one on me and it stung like hell. I was now mad. Honey must not knew that I've thrown down with the best of them. Don't let the looks fool you. She grabbed my hair and I gave her two short jabs. She stepped back and caught me in the jaw. Hard.She pushed and fell on top of me and damn near knocked me out of breath. She was twice my size.

"Bitch I'm finna beat yo ass hoe!" Honey said on top of me and snatched my top off, exposing my breast. I could see Oil Can and OG standing over us.

"Get her ass Lamira!" Jaden yelled from the background. "Beat that hoe ass!" I kneed her from the back and pushed her foward and got her off me, then made it on my feet first. I cauhgt her with a good punch in the mouth and nose. I side stepped and caught her in the ear. Honey was drunk from the blows and I twisted up a hand full of hair and gave her more blows to the face. "Bitch! I'll kill yo ass hoe! I'mma teach your stupid ass something bitch!" I said and threw her ass to the ground.

"Beat that hoe baby! "Oil can said getting it all on the camcorder."

"Youtube like a mothafucka!" OG annouced of his plans with the video.

"She needs a shirt!" Jaden said of my exposed chest.

"Fuck that shit! She straight! Beat that bitch baby!" Oil Can demanded with a kool-aid smile. I kicked her in the side and she crawled up in front of a twenty eight inch rim on the Hummer. Her face was bleeding and swollen and she spat some bloody spit.

"Bitch fuck you!" Honey said, throwing me the finger. I grabbed her by the hair and slapped her then spat in her face.

"T G Detail on Harding!" OG said pointing at the name that was made into the paint of the Hummer. "It's how we do! Trapstah for life! Tell'em Lamira!"

"Trapstah bitch!" I said to the camcorder. Oil Can handed me his chain with the house on it and I held it out towards the camcorder with titties and all showing.

"That's what's up!" OG took the camera as Oil Can hugged me from the back and held my hand in the air. Jaden had put Plies on the Cd changer and went to popping her ass like Ciara. OG handed Oil Can a bottle of Cristal. He took a sip and made me pour the rest on Honey. She got up and stumbled to her car. Then the camera went to Jaden and the Hummer.

Chapter 17
"Oil Can"

The video of Honey's ass kicking was the perfect advertisement, cause the shop was jumping. People was coming just to take pictures with the Hummer. I was standing in front of the detail part of the building lusting on this canary yellow Escalade on twenty fours with Gucci interior. The butterfly door's displayed its audio and entertainment componets. It was being detailed by two red-bones wearing short shorts and a t-shirt that had "TG's" on the back. We were having a calender shoot and a fundraiser for the Me-Me Foundation. All the detail employees at the moment were models. OG and Jaden was running things in perfect tune with each other. Ballers and businessmen lusted from the sidelines as their toys got cleaned. OG was the nigga in my eyes. He was handling his business. I've grown to respect him even more. Tiffany was standing beside me with Ms.Ann on the other side of her.

"I don't care *how* nice she is!" Tiffany screw faced me when I told her how nice Jaden was with kids, really doing it to fuck with her.

"Fa real though, she straight Tiff!" I said and she elbowed me and smacked her lips. "N-E-Way! Where is my chap stick at? Punk!" Tiffany said and was about the only girl that could get away with calling me a punk.

"Man you left that shit in my car two weeks ago, and N-E-way, don't jump off the subject. Why you hatin on Jaden?"

"I'm not hating on her. She's just rude! can't say excuse me." Tifffany said with her pretty eyes focused on OG.

"Okay, she accidently bumped you and she did say excuse me!" I said and looked at Ms.Ann. "And momma, you sitting there riding with her!"

"*And*?" Ms.ann said with a roll of the neck. "*And* she's probably on of your has beens!" That was Tiffany.

"Fa real!" Ms.Ann said and gave me a dirty look.

"N-E-Way!" I said and was cut off by Tiffany.

"Yeah nigga N-E-Way, OG is my *man*! I'm just letting his ass cleanse himself!" Tiffany claimed and thumped my arm.

"Man, I'm not about to let yall double team me with that *mess*!" I fanned them off and walked off to my freshly detailed Corvette.

"Ole dog!" Tiffany spat at my back.

"Nawl girl, mangy mutt!" Ms.Ann said and I heard a high five followed by some chuckling.

I went to Little Rock to meet up with my connect. I walked into their room which was church quiet. I smelled purple weed.

"What it is Texan Tino,Lil Paul?" I said giving both niggas dap. Texas Tino had them birds. Lil Paul had the weed. "What it is Oil Can? Nigga that's that 07 Vette ain't it?" Lil Paul said with nothing on but a white t-shirt and 8732 jeans.

"Bad mothafucka!" Texan Tino said in the same attire. Both had on Jordans.

"Ya'll niggas need to invest in ya boy! Nigga I does it big!" I said and fired up one of my blunts. If it wasn't with my brother,I smoked solo.

"What it is?" Texas Tino asked. "Ay, next trip, I wanna buy twenty five of them and fronted fifty at sixteen point five."

You got to be out yo mind! But since it's you my nigga, I'm ma fuck with you." Texas Tino said blowing weed out of his nose.

"You is good business my nigga." That was Lil Paul. He reminded me of a thugged out Will Smith with a Texas voabulary.

"Already!" I said blowing out smoke. I opened up the small platinum garbage can on my chain and dipped some powder out and sniffed it.

"I got some choppers for sale!" I advertised.

"Give me forty of'em! ASAP!" Texas Tino purchased and sipped some Hennesee straight out the bottle.

"Already! Ya'll wanna fuck something while yall here? Got some Latin candy for ya!" I said speaking of Maria and her click. I had met her through OG and already had hit. "Make it happen my nigga!" Texas Tino said.

Fa real!" Lil Paul cosigned.

<hr>

I went home and got some head from Lamira while reflecting on how much money, I was about to produce of the fifty on a front. That damn Hummer costed a pretty penny but OG wanted it. Lamira made some chili and as soon as I was about to get to eating OG called.

"Where you at?'

"At the house, what it is?" I asked getting a spoonful of chili up to my mouth.

"Pimp just got shot, meet us at Cool's trap!" OG said and the spoon went back into the bowl along with my appetite.

"Bet." I hung up. "Lamira, bring me that thang off the dresser." I said referring to my nine millimeter. I had a desert Eagle on me but it was too big for my outfit. Lamira brought the other pistol. "Everything alright?" She asked massaging my shoulders.

"Nawl! Pimp got shot! I thought you had something to tell

me? And why was you throwing up? You either sick or pregnant!" I said as my phone came to life again. "Nigga I'm on my way!" I said and hung up, knowing it was OG. "I gotta go, we'll talk about this tonight."

Everybody met up at Central Park, on the westside and we discussed the shooting. A Loot Dog had beaten Pimp to his pistol. Pimp still managed to let off two into the dude's chest and he was currently in Intensive Care. So we sent soliders to finish the job in case he talked or tried another attempt.

"Think we should call the party off?" OG asked as we were leaving.

"Nah, we straight. If that nigga Pimp wasn't high as fuck, he probably would have died." I said dropping the top on the Vettte.

"Who you telling!" OG said and fired up a blunt and putting Gorilla Zoe CD in.

"Man, this bitch Lamira acting funny." I said leaving the park heading to club Twenty Four.

"Fa real? How?" OG asked passing the blunt. "Man the bitch throwing up in the middle of the night, she don't throw that pussy on a nigga like she used to, then she be looking at a nigga all funny." I stopped at a light.

"Then they act like we ain't suppose to notice the difference." OG said.

"I think this hoe pregnant my nigga. Bitch scared to tell a nigga." I stated like it was a fact.

"Tiff say she used to do the same shit. Throwing up and throwing tantrums!" OG said taking the blunt.

"Well Imma ask this bitch tonight what her problem is! Ay, I got the plug to hook us up with fifty!" I said giving my friend some dap.

"Already!" OG gave a big smile.

Twenty minutes later we were greeting all the Trapstah Gangstas as they came through the door of club Twenty Four. TG VIP was throwing a party with over thirty strippers as entertainment. The only other women were Jaden and Lamira. Once everybody was in we got live. Cool set the weed and Extacy pills out along with lines of cocaine. You still had to buy drinks so the owner could make a little something. I was taking pictures with all of the strippers. The big homies in the joint was going to love these. I was taking shots with this thick ass redbone and a caramel appetizer when Lamira came up with a bottle of Cristal.

"Hey baby!" She smiled and pecked my lips.

"What it is?" I said palming redbone's ass, holding my pose. "I'm good!" Lamira said sipping her drink with both hands. "Damn she's thick! What's your name shawty?" She asked and eyed the candy.

"Red!" The stripper said smiling at Lamira.

"I like you Red! And it's evident my man does too. Holla at me later!" Lamira said to Red and rubbed her jawline. "Baby, I really got something to tell you!"

"*Fa real*, cause you been acting funny!" I said.

"I know, but I got you baby!" Lamira said and gave me some of her champagne. I took a big swig and finished up with the pictures. OG got on the mic.

"Everybody pay the fuck attention!" He said with Jaden by his side. "Trapstah Gangsta click is on the fise! We gettin money! So it was only right that we add a branch to our organization. I would like everybody to meet Jaden!" OG pulled Jaden close. "Most of ya'll know her as my girl but tonight she's officially The First Lady of The Trapstah Ladies!"

"That's what's up!" I yelled out having his back, knowing the click would follow. And they did. "Already!...."

"Fa real!...."

"Do it big then!...."

"Right now I need all the strippers in this bitch to come to life!" OG said as our theme song came to life. As every member of our click recited Trap or Die word for word, the strippers were down to thongs and tank tops with "TG" on them. While they popped their asses and dropped I made my way to OG with Lamira on my heels. OG and Jaden was throwing money on this peanut buttery beauty with braces. She was mopping the floor with her ass.

"What it is brah?" I said to OG and we did our hand shake. The Extacy pills had kicked in and I got emotional. "I love you brah. Fa real. I love you too Jaden. Ya'll love me? I know Lamira love me. You love me Lamira?" I looked at her and she smiled at me. OG was looking at me like I was crazy. I felt wierd. Like I was tired all of a sudden. I hugged them. "Ay, I'll be right back." I said and left the click to go to the bathroom. The bathroom was empty so I took a piss and then looked in the mirror as I washed my hands. My vision was blurry so I washed my face. I looked back up in the mirror and there was a nigga behind me with braids in his hair. I tried to turn around and caught a bullet in my left arm. I looked at my arm and then looked back up only to be staring down the barrel of a big ass pistol. I don't know why but I couldn't talk nor move. Not from being scared, but from some odd reason. Then all of a sudden my shooter's neck had exploded and the last thing I saw was OG standing over me. I passed out.

Chapter 18
"Lamira"

"We trap or die nigga!" All of the Trapstah Gangstas were yelling in unison as the strippers did their thing. Oil Can had just left to go to the restroom. I was organizer of the party and everything was going as planned. Which was the main reason I was standing beside Jaden and OG nervous as hell. Looking on the outside, I was having fun, but on the inside I was ready to get this over with. Jaden looked at me out the corner of her eye too quick for OG to notice when Oil Can went in the bathroom. I knew Oil Can and OG was smart enough to search the club before everybody made it and would greet everybody coming in. So I had hid an Eastside Piru in the ceiling before anyone made it. Jaden gave the owner and the bartender a lap dance while I snuck him in. Now Oil Can was about to give up the ghost. I had given him some of my champagne with drops of visine in it. I was faking like I was sipping from a straw. A minute passed and the party was crunk but my mind was in that restroom. Oil Can should be dead by now with old boy back in the ceiling. OG must've felt something because he stopped throwing money and went for the restroom. He went in and I saw a flash of light that happen three or four times before the door closed. The music was too loud to hear anything, so I gave Jaden a look that said I was heading that way. I saw a Trapstah go in the restroom and come out walking fast towards Cool who was coming up fast. I entered the restroom to see OG bent down in front of Oil Can. The Eastside Piru's neck was barely there as he laid in a pool of blood.

Dead.

"What the fuck going on bruh?" Oil Can asked in a drowsy state. His arm was bloody. "I'm dizzy as fuck!"

"Fuck!" OG shouted with his pistol still in his hand. "I done killed this nigga! My second mothafuckin murder conviction, how in the fuck I pose to tell Me-Me this shit? Huh?" OG brought Oil to his feet.

"Bruh, get me out of here. Nigga you saved my life, you know I'mma take the charge." Oil Can said leaning agaist OG's chest as OG held him up. Once again OG had got in my way. The first time was when I had cooked Oil Can some chili with poison in it, but as soon as he was about to eat, OG called and did something to his appetite. Now this.

"How the fuck did this nigga Get in here?" OG asked with the ultimate screw face. He turned to me. "Get the Vette ready!"

<hr />

OG and Cool toted Oil Can to the Vett, all the Trapstahs had their pistools out. The strippers were getting their asses out of there without clothes. Someone called the police cause we saw them on the highway as we headed to Jefferson Regional Medical Center. Jaden and I were in OG's Cadillac following him and Oil Can.

"Damn! What the fuck happen? You were suppose to hold that nigga!" I said to Jaden who had let OG go into the restroom.

"What the fuck was I suppose to do ? The nigga felt that shit!" Jaden said making the same left turn OG made. "Didn't he though! Fuck!" I shouted. "That Eastside nigga is dead! What the fuck we gonna tell them niggas? And then it was Motorcycle Man!" I exhaled. Hard.

"It is what it is Lamira, and I ain't trying to get killed. So we gonna handle it. We got to amp the game up. *Fuck crying about it!*"

"Already." I said as we turned in J.R.M.C. "What we gonna tell Popcorn?"

"Not shit! Cause we got to finish this shit!" Jaden said parking and cutting off the engine. We caught up with OG in the waiting room who was paranoid, watching everything that moved. "What happen baby?" Jaden asked OG. we were huddled in the corner. "I dunno, I just felt something up and found a nigga fuckin with brah!"

"How is he?" I asked OG with tears flowing facticiously somehow. I hugged him. "OG what's going on?"

"I dunno know, but that was close. Like an inside job." He exhaled and held a tear back from all most falling. "Alot of shit about to pop off *fa real.*" The tear fell. "It's gonna be a hot summer!" Two days later Oil Can and OG was on Pine Bluff's most wanted. Some of the strippers had got jammed up trying to leave and gave testimonies. Oil Can took the charge and turned himself in. Only five people knew the truth. Jaden, Oil Can, OG, Cool, and myself were the only people that knew OG was the shooter.

The Eastside Pirus would be looking for Jaden and I. We had gotten Motorcycle Man killed. I was curled up on the couch watching the local news. The strippers must have told too much because they named Oil Can and OG as leaders of the Trapstah Gang and that the shooting was gang related. It will be a few days before he gets a bond, if he gets one. The house phone rung and it was him calling from the county jail.

"Hey baby!" I sung in a worried tone.

"What it is?" "Nothin. Sitting here mad and lonely." I said and flipped through channels. I felt kind of gulity being that he had got shot and in jail for some shit I coordinated. And then I was staying in his place. "Ay, look, that nigga OG gone need you to play your position." Oil Can said and exhaled. "Ay, be here Tuesday. You aight?"

"Didn't I tell yo ass I was mad? Dang!" I said and smacked my lips. "I put some more money on your books."

"Why? I told yo ass not too! Six hundred is enough!"

"I dunno, shit I was bored and just had to do something!" I exhaled. "I miss you so much, what we gonna do?" I whined.

"Look shawty, I'm straight. Don't start that crying shit! Be Lamira the gangsta bitch!"

"Man, shut up!" I said and felt at ease for some odd reason.

"You get sick today?" Oil Can asked out the blue. "Nope. I'm alright I guess." I got up and went into the kitchen. "You miss me?"

"Ay, I miss you so much that I thought about you all day!" Oil Can said real cool.

"Ah yeah?" I said real feminine for him. "What about?"

"About how you don't think I know that you're hiding something from me!"

"What?" I said with a guilt that had my heart thumping like I was standing outside a Techno Club.

"You're pregnant. I've been around enough women to know. And you're at the stage to where you *been knew*." Oil Can said and it was quiet a split second. "See, and yo ass is too quiet which means I'm right. Yep. I learned you! Now put it on our love that you're not pregnant?" Oil Can tested and I couldn't do it. I stood there looking stupid. "Why did you hide that?" Oil Can asked still cool. "Baby, I'm scared!" I searched for a little sympathy.

"Don't be." He got quiet, then exhaled. "Look, you good so don't trip. Work with my brotha. I'll call you back tomorrow."

"Alright. I love you!" I said before I thought it. I was tripping.

"Aight." Was all Oil Can said and hung up.

Chapter 19
"OG"

They were tripping on giving Oil Can a bond and the click was too busy to help me organize both sides of our enterprise. So I needed Jaden to run the business aspect. I had to meet with the connect to ensure that we would still get fifty on front with Oil Can in jail. He had to do the jail shit this time. What was a trip out of the whole situation was that the nigga that tried to hit Oil Can was from the Eastside Piru's. I had raised the nigga shirt up checking for affilliation and sure enough he had ESP on his chest. I knew they were coming sooner or later. what I want to know is how did the guy get in? I was going to find out but right now, I had to run the organization. The connect let me know that it was all good with the work, so I rented a room in Houston, Texas where we met up and chilled for a second. When they left I called Me-Me.

"Hey baby!" I said after she answered on the first ring with attitude.

"Nothing dad." Malicia said wanting me to hear it in her voice.

"Man, what's wrong?"

"What's going on with my uncle? Why won't nobody tell me?" Malicia said and exhaled.

"Baby don't worry, everything is straight. He just in jail." I said and Oil Can's business phone vibrated. "Hold on Me-Me. What it is?"

"Say brah, this Stay Puff, G, it's raining down here in the s-dub. What it is?"

"what it is? This OG."

"Awe, what up OG! Where Oil Can?" Stay Puff G asked.

"He on some mo shit but I got you. Can you drop top?' I asked what he wanted.

"Yeah in bout an hour, I'll have two white girls with me!" Stay Puff G said wanting two birds. "Holla at Cool at McD's on Main." I said.

"Already." Stay Puff G said and hung up.

"Me-Me-." I said to the other phone.

"As long as your name is Octavious Green, don't ever put me on hold like that!"

"My bad." I exhaled and needed a break from all the stress. "Where yo momma?"

"Which one?" Malicia said of Tiffany and momma.

"Momma momma." I said firing up a blunt.

"She went shopping and she's in your Hummer! You see Barrak on CNN last night?" Malicia asked.

"Nawl, I missed him, did he show out?"

"Yes! But dad I got to go, I'm showing momma how to tie a Chinese knot." Malicia said. "Aight baby, be good."

"Love you daddy!" Malicia said still upset with me.

"Love you too."

—◄◉►—

"Brah, the nigga just came up out of nowhere!" Oil Can was telling me. He was in Pulaski County due to Pine Bluff's jail was full, being the murder rate was at an all time high. "Man, how the nigga get in? That was some inside shit!" I said. "I saw that nigga and let loose!" "Already." Oil Can cosigned. "Ay, there she go" Oil Can nodded his head towards a female guard. "She works my pod all the time. Go and fuck her for me brah so she'll handle up."

"Already my nigga, already." I said eyeing her thickness. "But look, I had Cool grab some soliders and kidnap the bartender, owner, and the DJ for a little torture."

"Them niggas been on us for a minute my nigga!" Oil Can said of the Eastside Pirus. "They already knew about the party. They either was already in their hidden, or let in after the greeting!"

"Fa real!" I concurred.

"It is what it is." Oil Can said and I knew exactly what he meant. We had to attack first as a scare tatic. "I don't think they can handle the pressure. Send a chopper through."

"I'm on it."

Our thirty minutes were up, so we said our departures and I jammed ole girl up.

"Ay, my nigga speaking highly of you and that's rare being that he don't know you. What it is, what's your name?"

"Sandy, and yours?" Sandy said with a nice voice. I knew she knew who I was, me and Oil had been on the news for two days. But I played her game. "I'm OG, and before we go any futher I must say that you have a nice voice! And then you got some pretty ears!"

"What?" Sandy blushed and giggled. "Thick and shit!" I mumbled under my breath but clear enough for her to hear.

"You are *too* much!" She laughed and touched my arm.

"Let me *show* you much, kick it with a nigga." I said and like that I had her number and picked her up after work.

⋙⋘

Sandy was now sitting on the passenger side of the STS waiting on me to come out of my apartment. I had came to tell Jaden to cancel the photo shoot. She was sitting indian stlye on the bed with her lap top and eating strawberries.

"Why? I can handle it." Jaden said with her glasses on making her more sexy.

"Cause I need you on some more shit."

"Okay. Oh, Me-Me called. She wants to do dinner." Jaden said and stood up on the bed to stretch. She had on a sky blue and red panty and bra set and a silk robe hanging off her shoulders.

"When? Tomorrow?" I asked and thought of Tiff if she was to see Jaden and Me-Me doing dinner.

"Yeah, about six. Where you headed now, I want to be held baby! I miss you!" Jaden seductively whined. Her braces caught the light and twinkled. "I got this girl in the car now I got to fuck for Oil Can, she work at the county. So if you have time baby, get a prepaid phone, MP3, a quarter pound of some weed and an ounce of powder."

"Already sweetheart!" Jaden grabbed a packet off the night stand. "And put it on her, so she takes care of bruh." Jaden said walking up on me standing on the edge of the bed. I kissed her navel. She pushed an Ex pill in my mouth and gave me the packet with more. "Go her Tiger!"

———◦《◉》◦———

"Them niggas didn't know shit!" Cool said over the phone talking about the owner,DJ,and the bartender." And I believe them cause they died saying it. We injected pure Herion in their system and left them in a motel room in West Helena."

"Damn. Shit aint looking right!" I said.

"That leaves two options, the click or them hoes." Cool said but something still wasn't right."I think the nigga was already in the club." I said.

"Fa real, and it wasn't a Trapstah that let him in, nor a stripper." Cool said and I knew what he meant. "We'll figure it out my nigga,for now, send a chopper to spray them niggas hood." I said. "Already."

I went to the shop and discussed it with momma and Tiffany. We sat in my office while Jaden and Latunda ran the shop. Tiffany was giving me much attitude about having Jaden relieve her. "I don't know son, but I would suggest you watch yourself." Momma said. "And it's someone closer than you know!"

"I wouldn't be surprise if it's Ms. Thang!" Tiffany mumbled towards her folded arms. "Tiff. you know what? You need to check yo self. Fa real!" I said, sick of her little attitude.

"Fuck you!" Tiffany spat out.

"In ya mothafuckin mouth!" I screw faced her.

"Tiff! Octavious!" Momma snapped and gave us a face that made us get right.

"N-E-Way, I don't want ya'll working the shop right now, it's not safe." I ordered.

"What?" Tiffany asked knowing damn well she heard me.

"You heard me didn't you momma? Tell Tiff!" "And where am I suppose to work?" Momma asked as she sat on the edge of the couch. Tiffany followed suit.

"With Tiff at the foundation." I said. "Boy please! I'm more gangsta that half of these Wangstas out here!" Momma said. Frontin' of course. "Momma!" I gave her my look of not playing. "Alright, Alright. I guess it's back to the projects playing cards!" Momma said now playing with Tiffany hands. Tiffany was staring at me like an enemy.

"And I wish you *would* let them go out to dinner!" Tiffany roared. Momma chuckled and Tiffany gave her a look that made her stop.

"Why is you fucking with me?" I said heated. Tiffany rolled her eyes and smacked her lips.

"Excuse us momma." Tiffany said and momma left the room.

"Quit fucking with me Tiff!" I said in her face. She tried to get up but I pushed her back down. "Move! Punk!" She shouted. I let her up and she got in my face. "Fuck you OG! Why you keep disrespecting me?" "Man! Shut that shit up!" I screw faced her, but she was not intimidated at all, with her pretty self. She stared at me for a second.

"You need to watch them females OG." She said in a quiet tone only I could hear. "*They* can become close enemies. If not Already."

"Your saying that cause you don't like them!" I defended for another answer.

"You can be so stupid at times! Damn!" Tiffany said with a smirk. I could tell she wanted to cry. "Man, fuck you!"

"Fuck you nigga!" Tiffany spat back and we kissed for no reason. I looked at her looking at my lips and we done it again but this time like lovers. Past memories flooded my mind of us when we was one. It felt so natural as if our hearts were beating *as one*. I missed her so much I now realized. Her kiss was better than anything in the world right now. Jaden open the door and caught us. I now realized that we were holding each other.

"I'll be out in a minute." I said to Jaden and she shut the door without a word. We stood there not wanting to let each other go. I put some loose hair behind her ear. "I still love you Tiff, no matter what." I said staring into her pretty eyes. "N-E-Way, remember what I told you." Tiffany said breaking our embrace.

We left the office. Tiffany looked at Jaden with a his-ass-is-still-mines smile. Jaden smirked and chuckled to herself. "What's up?" I said to Jaden at one of the registers.

"What's up boo!" She said cool and easy. "You aight?" I asked giving her arm a soft squeeze. "Damn braces!" Jaden said and gave a pretty customer her reciept. "Didn't I tell you not to disrepect me?

Let me know things before they happen so I won't be in the blind."

"That shit in there just happened." I said and meant.

"Okay, I know that's baby momma and all, but she better stay the fuck out of my way!" Jaden said and meant.

Chapter 20
"Tiffany"

"You go girl!" Ms.Ann said and we high fived. She wanted me as her daughter in law over anyone else.

"And Ms.Jaden caught yall?"

"Yes!" I smiled at the memory. "And that shit felt good!" We were in a corner of the shop watching Jaden and OG talk. "I'm telling you momma, something ain't right about her."

"Yeah, I can feel it to, but OG can handle himself." Ms.Ann said eyeing a customer's cute little outfit with matching sandles.

"Nu unh, I got my man's back! I love him so much momma and that kiss lets me know that we belong together!" I smiled more to myself than at her. "I saw you kissing my man!" Jaden said with a smirk after we strolled up to the registers. I can't hate, her eyebrows were perfect.

"And I apologize cause it wasn't suppose to happen."

"No need. Why? Cause you don't like me anyway!" Jaden said sacking up the customer's purchase. "You know what though, it's all good cause you're his baby momma and he can tap that ass anytime! I don't give a fuck, just stay the fuck out of my way!" Jaden finish real cute. "Hold up! No you didn't go there with your rude ass!" I screw faced her.

"Look, I'm a boss bitch! I'll have you knocked off while I'm brushing my teeth! Now. Get the fuck out my face!" Jaden said non-chalant as if she meant it. And it kind of scared me. I looked at Latunda at the other register who was trying to mind her own business but this scenario was getting good. Jaden looked at me and smiled. "Will you be purchasing anything today mamm?" She said with a feminine wink. I gave her a fuck you stare and turned to leave and ran smack into OG. I took advantage of some get back. I grabbed his face and gave him a big smack on his lips. Before he could respond I turned around to Jaden and gave her the same wink back.

———— ◆ ————

I went home only to get into it with Neko.

"I told you not to smoke that shit in my house! Damn!" I said rubbing my temples. "You know what Tiffany, your ass has been complaining all fuckin week. Actin like you on yo period or something!" Neko fussed shutting the window! "You know what? This is too much!" I said more to myself.

"You need to get yo shit together!" Neko said getting up in my face. "Yo pussy ain't that good no mo, you always crying about nothing, and don't think I don't know you chasing yo baby daddy!"

"What?" I frowned up at his punk ass.

"Callin the nigga name in ya sleep! You think about him when we fuck?" Neko asked sarcastically.

"Nigga fuck you!" I shouted and started crying. "Get the fuck out! Now!"

"Bitch!" Neko shouted and picked me up by my neck. I grabbed the curling iron on the dresser and popped him in the eye. He threw me across the room onto the bed.

"Punk ass nigga!" I threw the curling iron and cracked my dresser mirror. "You gonna put yo mothafuckin hands on me?" I beated my chest. "OG gone fuck, you, up!"

"Fuck you *and* that nigga OG! That nigga better be worried about them Piru niggas!"

An hour later Neko was gone and I was on the couch with the only two friends I had. MS.Ann and Me-Me.

"But momma, he started it!" I said of the fight.

"That is not right momma," Malicia butted in, "you started with the smoking!" I rolled my eyes at her. "So what's it going to be? Ya'll calling it quits?" Ms.Ann said painting her toenails on the other end of the couch. She had on some short shorts and a tank top looking nineteen years old. "Hell yeah, he put his hands on me! And yall better not tell OG cause he will kill that fool!" I said and stared at Me-Me.

"Alright momma I'm not going to say nothing!" She rolled her eyes. "Dang!" She slapped my arm and I looked at her like she was crazy. "You didn't tell me you kissed daddy!"

"Big mouth ass!" I accused Ms. Ann and conviction was written all over her face. "I'll tell you about it later. Let me tell you about Ms. Jaden. I don't trust her and my instints tells me she has something to do with that shooting. Especially after what she told me today. Her and her friend ain't right and now I'm on they ass. Plus I'm about to claim what's mine, cause that kiss made me melt! Whew!" I reminisced and my panties got soaked for the fourth time today. I was now on a mission to get Jaden's ass out the way.

Chapter 21
"Lamira"

"D o it again!" Oil Can threatened about me putting more money on his books. I put five hundred more on there this morning.

"Man, shut up! Hell, it's my money anyway!" I said and smacked my lips I was at the county jail visiting him, I could see weight loss in his face from my side of the visiting window. "If they don't give you a bond me and Jaden gonna shoot up the court house like that book *Dutch*! Fa real!"

"Already! Where this nigga OG at? Nigga should have *been* here!" Oil Can said and no sooner than he said it OG embraced me from behind with Jaden on his heels.

"Let me holla at my brah!" OG said bogarding the window. "What it is nigga? You get that?" "Already, preciatte that brah!" Oil Can said from his side of the glass and put his fist on it. OG dapped it from his side. "Hey Oil Can baby!" That was Jaden. She blew him a kiss. I smelled her strawberry lip gloss. "I be glad when your ass get out, me and Lamira gonna suck your dick at the same time!"

"Already!" I said seductively. "Baby I need some dick!"

"OG got you!" Oil Can said and I smirked at him and OG.

"Yeah right! I *been* trying to get it from him. N-E-Way, I want yours!" I somehow made myself flush over and I think I had him hypnotized for a minute. "That's what's up!" Oil Can said and nodded at OG for them to talk. Jaden and I eased onto our on space.

"I think this nigga baby momma is going to be a problem. I could tell by the looks I been getting from her." Jaden said as if it came from her deepest thoughts.

"And then she nosey as hell!" I said feeling the material of her shirt. "Fuck it, have that hoe knock off too!"

"I hope you know that the Eastside Pirus are looking for us." Jaden warned and I noticed a hint of fear in her face.

"They will probably be all over Fayetteville looking for us!" I said.

"*And* here in the Bluff." Jaden said and looked at me. "We got to knock this nigga OG off to spare our lives!" "*And* get the connect!" I said now realizing the seriousness of the situation. I exhaled.

"OG says that two Trapstah Gangstas got shot up last night. That he had that nigga Cool go spray up their hoods. This shit so silly. N-E-Way, how is we going to take OG out?" Jaden asked. "Which ever way, It's gonna have to be some helluva shit!" I said looking over at OG knowing good and damn well it would be easier for me to whoop a full grown lion than to try and kill this man. But now it was kill or be killed and how it got this serious, I did not know.

We left and went to the apartment Oil Can had in Little Rock in which I was staying in. OG and JAden started playing with each other. I had noticed in the car on the way here that OG had looked at us strange a few times. Especially when he thought I wasn't looking. So I brought up the shooting.

"They had to be some slick mothafuckas!" I said out of nowhere.

"Who that?" Jaden asked when OG took off his shirt. "However dude got in, he must've hid in the ceiling or something. I'm just saying" I revealed as a tactic to make it seem as if I'd discovered something new to the puzzle.

"Ay, you might be on to something." OG said in a tone that said he damn near knew who did it. I broke a light sweat.

"And that was a real close call." Jaden said trying a different approach to get the tension off what I just said. "I've invested *too much* into this empire to see it fall."

"That's what's up!" OG said wrapping himself around Jaden. I sat at the bar and twisted up a blunt. OG phone rung. "Yeah,yeah,fa real? Fuck!" OG hung up and rubbed his temples. "Cool just got murked!"

———⦅◉⦆———

We shot to some town called Humphrey and was posted in a field with some trailors. All the Trapstah Gangstas were in a meeting and with Jaden and I as head ladies of Trapstah Ladies, we were allowed to attend. Cool had been killed by some Eastside Pirus that had spotted him puming gas and kidnapped him. They then tied him up and cut his fingers and toes off and he bled to death. Then an AK47 shooting van came flying through Trapstah hood and tossed the body. Trapstah Gangstas was also about to launch a record label. Especially with the media hype that they were recieving right now. The video of me kicking Honey's ass had made me some what of a celebrity. Shit was getting hected. And I was seeing another side of OG.

"Everybody need a couple of shooters with them at all times! And it's trap or die with me!" OG said to his congregation and amens went through it. "Nigga it's war time and we got the most choppas! And that's what's up!"

We left and went to the shop to let Jaden catch up on some paperwork on the models' contracts. OG and I hopped in the Hummer. There was a car following us loaded with guns. No way a person could dodge all those bullets. This was being bold of us to be out and on our way to Wal-Mart. OG had a big ass gun on him and I had a

P223 in my purse. "I know what I want to do for my next shoot!" I said with a girly face.

"What it is?" OG said getting on Hardin Street.

"Cheerleader outfit with knee high stills!"

"That's what's up! Show them pretty legs!" OG said and then ran his big hand down my thigh. My pussy jumped. He slapped it and I damn near came. "OG I'm horny as fuck!" I confessed as we strolled down the four lanes."My insides are about to explode!"

"Then jack off!" OG recommended with a look as if to say that he was serious. "Nigga please! I want some dick!" And with that said I reached over and grabbed OG's zipper and reached in and got what I'd been craving for the last two weeks. His dick felt so natural in my mouth as I devoured it. He got into it and ran his hands through my hair.

"Damn shawty! Yo shit is the truth!" OG moaned and manuevered the Hummer into Wal-Mart parking lot. And then he parked quicker that usual. I slobbered and made it juicy for him then went at it with no hands. I quickly got my shorts and thong to my knees and sat on OG's dick sideways with my legs on the passenger seat. OG was lifting me up and down on his big dick and I came damn near four times before he got his first one. My ass was on fire. And being inside Wal-Mart didn't make it no better. My pussy was throbbing and I thought once or twice about gong in the bathroom to play with my clit. OG purchased the cell phone he was getting for his daughter and we went to U.A.P.B. To give it to Tiffany the porcelian doll. The bitch that was in our business.

The bitch Jaden plans to knock off.

After we handle OG. I was dropped off at Oil Can's place so I could get ready for the photo shoot. I had a strange feeling in my gutt that made me nervous when I first stepped into the house. I pulled out my gun and eased through the house for any surprises. The house was silent except for the tick of the clock on the wall. The house came up clean. I thought about OG and our sexual encounter. I envied Jaden. and Oil Can's bond hearing is in the morning, so I could've waited one more day for some dick. But it was the perfect opportunity to taste that chocolate!

The doorbell rung and brought me out my thoughts and replaced it with a paranoia state. I grabbed my gun and looked out the peephole at a pimpled face white boy.

"Yes?" I asked. "Melody's balloon and confetti! You have ballons! There from Javon!" Pimple man said.

"Aww! Oil Can sent them!" I smiled opening the door. He moved the ballons and my heart fell in my ass. Popcorn smiled at me.

Then all of a sudden a hand behind me held a rag to my mouth and snatched me back in the house. Some strong odor came from the rag that caused me to pass out.

"Hey there! I been looking for you! How have you been?" Popcorn smiled moving some hair out of my face. I was slowly coming to life. I felt weak. I was laying on my stomach and it felt like my legs were open. I tried to turn over and realized I was tied to the bed. Naked.

"What's going on?" I started to panic. "Popcorn please, just hear me out. I don't know what happened but OG intercepted and he's the shooter!"

"Ah yeah?" Popcorn said sacastically and nodded to another guy in the room. Demon and two other dudes were present. I looked around to see what was going on.

"And the connect?" Demon asked behind me as somebody inserted a rod like object in my pussy. "We got it!" I lied trying to buy time. Whatever it was inside of me was getting warm. "Got to get the number out his phone that OG has and it's yours!" The object got hot and I now realized that they had a curling iron inside me. It got so hot I screamed out of nowhere. I had never felt that type of pain in my life.

"You think this shit is a joke don't you? Yall hoes trying to play us!" Demon yelled over my screaming. He yanked it out and burnt me on my shoulder. I screamed in agony. I smelled the aroma of burnt flesh. I couldn't believe this was happening. I was in safe hands an hour ago. Now this.

"Please! Please Popcorn!" I begged for mercy.

"Bitch! Shut the fuck up!" Popcorn slapped me and ole boy stuck the curling iron at the entrance of my stuff. All I could do was scream and endure the pain.

"When you fuck us you end up getting fucked!" Demon said and got naked. He put on a condom, grabbed some vaseline and slapped a pile in my ass. He jammed two fingers in my ass which hurted like hell. He then jammed his dick in my ass and I yelled. His dick was to big for a pussy let alone an asshole. The pain was inbearable and I past out. I was awakened immediately with some cold water to the face. My ass was being ripped apart and was halfway numb. Demon was going from tip to balls as I laid there and took it. I somehow knew I would die and said fuck it.

"Fuck all ya'll punk mothafuckas!" I said, numb from pain.

"Not before we fuck you!" Popcorn said and somebody sprayed Achohol in my ass and it burned beyond measure. I wanted to past out again but couldn't. Demon grabbed my hair and started fucking me like crazy. I prayed that God made it stop but to no avail.

Demon punched me in the back so hard that I think he broke my spine. I felt a sting from my neck down to my toes when Demon got off me and untied me. I couldn't move nothing but my eyes. They turned me over and my body was lifeless but full of tingles. One of the dudes in the room took a steak knife and carved something in my forehead. I tried to scream and holler but had lost my voice to low wails of pain. Then somebody produced a hammer and I was hit in the head. Then again. Then vivid pictures of my my life flashed in my head. The first time I left home as a teenager. My momma telling me about my period. My little brother.

The next thing I knew I was on my back in a hole. I could taste dirt. Then I started breathing it. It became hard to breath for a minute then I felt like I was suffocating. After that I felt sleepy and drifted that way.

Chapter 22
"Oil Can"

"Yeah, I'mma call, fa real!" I told Sandy. I had made OG fuck her for me and she became my horse. I didn't get any sleep in here cause most nights I was up snorting and talking on the cell.

"I'm fa real Oil Can. Don't bullshit me!" Sandy said. She was model material and down for a nigga so I might let her be a Trapstah Lady.

OG, momma, Ms.Ann, Tiffany, and Me-Me were waiting in a limo outside the jail along with reporters. Me and my Attorney came out and cameras was flashing just as the questions came. "Is it true you're head of Trapstar?..."

"Is Trapstar at war with other gangs?..."

"What changes will your freedom bring?..."

I got in the limo after my lawyer. After discussing further court issues, he got out and left.

"Hey boy!" My real momma said hugging me like crazy and acting as if she didn't just see me yesterday.

"What it is momma?" I said tapping her arm.

"You already getting on my nerves!" She said and grabbed Ms. Ann's arm as she laughed.

"With all that tapping!" That was Ms. Ann. She was imitating me by tapping Tiffany's arm.

"I want to know what's going on!" Malicia said sitting there looking grown with her legs crossed. "It ain't nothing." I said and pinched her jaw. Me-Me was my daughter too.

"There you go!" She said and rolled her eyes. "I want to know tonight. So call me, get my number from daddy."

"Already!" I turned to OG who knew what I wanted to ask and he gave me the I-don't-know shoulder hunch. Where was Lamira. As soon as we got off county grounds Trapstahs came out of nowhere, and probably with enough ammunition to start a middle east Malitia.

"Man, I got a bad feeling my nigga. Fa real. We shouldn't be in this limo with fam." I said to OG and the car got quiet at my seriousness.

"I got heat surrounding us brah. Plus the limo bullet proof. I got it in Texas from some nigga in Oak Cliff." OG said and asked me the question I had asked him. "Where's Lamira?" He asked, but for the summary of what I think done happen. "Ben Grimes." I said. Ben Grimes meant a kidnapping.

"Fa real? A Ben Grimes?" OG asked of my assumption. "Stacks on deck?"

"Stacks on deck." I said of a ransom. But nine times out of ten They'll kill her anyway. And we left it at that, the Eastside Pirus had kidnapped Lamira, and was holding her for ransom. If not already dead. "Why Eastside Pirus? What connection is there?" OG asked of what could tie Lamira to Trapstah. "Probably through the fight on youtube or the DVD." I said and exhaled. "Something ain't right my nigga."

———— ((O)) ————

The women went their seperate ways and I was on my way to

Memphis to meet the connect. OG was on the passenger with Pimp in the back and we were reminiscing on Cool. "Hell yeah! You talking bout the time that nigga damn near shot his own car up!" OG said. "Nigga damn near hit me in the foot one night!" Pimp said with more hurt in his eyes than anybody. Cool was his right hand man.

"Ya'll niggas know what?" I asked wheeling the rented Surburban through traffic. "That nigga Cool was Trapstah all the way, and for that, all ESP, LOOT, and any other click that want it, gonna get it!"

"Already!" OG and Pimp said in unison. We met up with the connect and was given the ok to send the horse to pick it up. They requested some company so we had Jaden to hook them up and send them some strippers. We went to Pure Passion and made it rain for a minute while we discussed issues of our organization.

"Nigga this fifty gonna get our ass in. Plenty to clean." OG said throwing his money at this blond redbone in our VIP section.

"Fa real." I cosigned. "Them niggas is gonna want to talk about it once half of their click is murked. What it is?" I looked at OG then at Pimp. "Fuck them niggas! It is what it is!" That was Pimp. Sometimes I forget that he was a straight up killer.

"Already! They took my nigga Cool!" OG said pumping money on blondie.

"Fa real!" I said throwing money on this thick yellowbone with braids to her ass. I went back to Lamira. "They got her don't they?"

"I think so brah." OG said knowing exactly what I felt. Lamira had brought money in by playing her position, and was about to really come up through Trapstah Ladies.

"What up with Jaden?" I asked. "She been hiding shit but I think it's some personal shit. Like, her hiding her kid from a nigga." OG said and ordered more champagne.

"Lamira was pregnant and could've ran off but for what reason I don't know." I said and deleted the thought. I felt what I already knew. Lamira was dead.

———— ≈«◉»≈ ————

Business was good and dope was moving. I went to the hood with Pimp riding shotgun to discuss these contracts with the record label OG wants to launch. Trapstah Records was about to fall into the media along with the Trial. I eased through West Meadows as soldiers greeted me from their post. We were holding it down against two clicks.

"Ay, this nigga on the East want four and a baby." Pimp said after talking code on the phone. "Where the nigga at?" "Off Ohio Street by the pawn shop." Cool said dialing another number to get the dope ready. "Already, I been wanting to holla at that Indian piece anyway!" I said ready to fuck something. My ring tones came to life on my personal and business cell. I answered the business first and handled it. I had missed the personal call and called back. It was Tiffany. "Brah, I don't trust that bitch Jaden!" She said in a whisper.

"There you go."

"Man fa real, something ain't right Oil." Tiffany said and I knew she was serious cause she called me Oil.

"I feel something to sis, but we just can't go accusing, that girl, that *is* OG's woman Tiff." "Nigga that's my man! And I'm tired of this shit! I thought you had my back brah?" Tiffany sounded as if she was about to whisper cry.

"Why you whispering?" I asked turning into the parking lot of a E-Z Mart. I had missed my turn. "Cause I'm looking at OG's punk ass smiling all in this bitch face! I'm hid in the back of McDonald's watching them at a table."

"Tiff! You stalking them? Get'cho crazy ass out of there before you piss OG off!" I said heated at her for doing that crazy ass shit.

"Man, I'm trying to." "Now!" I cut her off. She smacked her lips.

"Punk!" And then she hung up.

I finally went home after handling the business and gathering something to fuck. At my house I had soldiers on post and couldn't wait to indulge into these two peanut buttery delights that were girlfriends. They automatically knew who I was and would do anything to be down with Trapstah. My current drama was making me a celeb. I took a break after our first session to hit a line. I went to take a piss and chewed another Extacy pill. I was about to wash my hands when I spotted something in the sink. Lamira's phone. I picked it up and it displayed the missed calls. Out of eleven calls only one stood out. An unidentified Pine Bluff number. I called the number back.

No answer. I went back in the bedroom and my sex dolls were eating each other. My dick jumped back hard and I was ready to get in where I fit in. I sat the phone on the dresser and no sooner than I climbed on the bed, Lamira's ring tone kicked on.

"What it is?" I said playing with my dick, eyeing the pussy on the bed. "You miss her nigga?" A voice asked with a voice disquising chip.

"Who the fuck is this?" I asked as my erection went down.

"Nigga I asked you a question!"

"What the fuck ya'll want!" I asked now mad and grinding my teeth. "Get the fuck out!" I yelled at the freaks. They gathered their belongings and was gone.

"Listen nigga!" The voice said then I heard some moans of agony and dispair. Then there was a scream. "Javon! Help!" A voice said similar to Lamira's but with a lot of pain. It had to be her because she was always calling me by my government. "A hundred thou nigga! Tomorrow night, behind Jack Robey Jr. High. And don't try no funny shit or we murking this bitch!" The voice hung up and the house was at total silence. The ring tone kicked on again. "and bring the phone!" The voice said and hung up.

———≈《》≈———

"And the killing part about it brah is that it wasn't them Eastside niggas. They wouldn't have hid their voice. They would've wanted us to know." I said to OG. I went straight to his apartment after the call. Jaden was in the kitchen cooking.

"Yeah they would have. Loot Dogs?" OG asked passing me a blunt.

"I dunno. She worth the hundred stacks though, I'll get it back out of her ass." I said hitting the blunt then dipped into my garbage can on my neck. Jaden came out the kitchen with tears in her eyes.

"I can't believe this shit! Mothafucka! Some mothafucka is gonna have to pay!" She said on the verge of breaking down. "Come here baby!" OG said patting his lap and she abided. Her ring tone kicked in.

"Hello? What? Who is this? How did you get my number and why? Bitch!" Jaden hung up and gave OG the screwface. "How the fuck did Tiffany get my number?"

"I dunno." OG said with the screwface. "Talking about she don't want me staying here, and that she see through me!" Jaden jumped up. "I'm bout to go whoop her OG!"

"Girl, sit yo ass down! Now!" OG said and she abided back in the same spot. "We got to get this girl Lamira!"

"Damn!" I said and exhaled. I took the blunt. "Well I'mma handle it, I got them contracts in the truck."

"That's what's up." OG said and kissed Jaden on the neck.

"Let me check this food!" Jaden jumped up and ran in the kitchen. I gave OG a look as if who he'd put his money on if Tiff and Jaden were to fight.

"Jaden!" OG said. I agreed.

Jaden was sprawled out on top of the freshly detailed Hummer doing a photo shoot. There was a Bently and a Ferarri next in line to be touched by her body. She had on a two piece Louis Vutton swim suit and had my dick on the rise like Chris Brown's career. After the shoot Jaden came over to me.

"Please get my sister, I miss her so much!" She said and dropped her head so I couldn't see the tears form. She sniffled and threw her hair back and then wiped her tears. I knew then that she honestly didn't know what was up.

"I'mma handle it. You was looking good up there!" I said tapping her arm.

"I seen you lusting nigga! Aight now!" Jaden said seductively but cool at the same. OG and I left and got the money from under my uncle's pitbull doghouse and shot back to my place. I did a line and popped a bottle of champagne.

"Brah, look what we done built!" I said as we both watched CNN. OG had started me to paying attention to the world outside of ours.

"Nigga we got a major enterprise jumping!" OG said.

"Nigga I'm glad you stuck to yo plans! We got damn near two hundred thou in assets. And then with all our loot we still gettin Hood rich!" I said sipping my drink. "By the way, give me Malicia's number, I was suppose to call yesterday."

"That girl been texting me all day! Damn text Queen!" OG said and we shared a laugh. Then Lamira's ringtone put me back on point. The voice gave us instructions on which route to take to get to J.R.J.H.

I pulled into the empty parking lot and sat for a minute. "Go to the apartments behind the school, drop the bag in the bathroom of apartment twelve." The voice said after that minute. We left and went to the apartments. I parked.

"Hold me down brah, if I ain't back in five, come for me." I said putting my Desert Eagle on my hip and grabbing the duffle bag of money.

"Already." OG said and we did our hand shake. I walked up to apartment twelve and the phone came to life.

"Go in." The voice instructed. The apartment showed signs of habitants but vacant at the moment. Only one light was on and that was in the hallway. I assumed it was the bathroom. "Leave the money in the bathroom." The voice instructed again. I pulled out my gun and slowly made my way. The bathroom was small and I sat the duffle bag in front of the toilet. I smelled a familiar perfume and couldn't place it. I exhaled and turned to leave and was shocked to see what was before my eyes. I was looking down the barrel of a P223 and now knew who the perfume belonged too.

Chapter 23
"OG"

I was about to change the CD from BG to Rick Ross when it came to mind that five minutes had passed. I got out and went up to the apartment wondering what had transpired of the situation. I made it to the apartment not knowing rather to knock or what. I knocked and when no one answered I twisted the doorknob and let myself in. I felt death in the air plus the aroma of burnt bullets shells. The apartment was furnished but empty. I looked into a bedroom and called Oil's name. I moved on down and opened a hall closet. I called Oil's name again and walked toward a light and pushed the door opened.

My heart touched my toes.

Oil Can was laying on his back with thick blood running out the side of his mouth. There was a hole under his eye, another by his mouth, and one in his neck bleeding. His eyes were wide open. "Fuck!" I ran to his side and held his head in my hands. "Brah! Brah! Get up Brah!" I was crying like a bitch. Then I got mad. "Nigga get up! You bet not die! Nigga get up! Brah!" Oil Can blinked his eyes. "It's gonna be alright brah! Nigga get up!" I pulled out my phone and dialed 911 and told them the business. "Brah they on the way nigga we gonna make it!" I said and he started pumping too much blood through the hole in his neck and then stopped breathing. I yelled to the top of my lungs and started breathing hard with my screwface on. Staring at nothing in particular. My bestfriend and brother had just died in my arms. I closed his eyes.

I had managed to get my gun and Oil's hid in the car before the police came. I called momma and Tiffany. After the police did their invesigating and took the body, I met back up with the fam at my apartment. Everybody was in a frenzy crying and shouting. Jaden woke up out of her sleep and came to my aid trying to help me calm everybody. She didn't even know what was going on.

"Oil just got killed." I said fighting back my anger.

"What?" Jaden whispered with tears welling up in her eyes. "Oh my God! What happened? Where's Lamira?" Jaden asked now in a panic.

"I dunno. Shit is fucked! Shit is all fucked! My mothafuckin brah is gone. Jaden he gone!" I said breaking down.

"Baby it's alright!" Jaden said holding me. I was getting mad all over again. Tiffany jumped up and came to me.

"Move Jaden, he need me!" Tiffany said and tried to hold me. "Octavious!" She weeped.

"Tiffany, right now is not the time!" Jaden explained in a calm tone.

"Bitch, this is my mothafuckin man!" Tiffany yelled in her face and took one on her. Jaden took the punch and sidestepped, and gave Tiffany two quick ones that made her knees buckle. She quickly gained her balance back and I put my back to Jaden and put my hand around Tiffany's neck.

"What the fuck wrong with you?" I asked then released her. "You gon' pick this bitch over me?" Tiffany yelled at me crying with a sideways glance. Her lips were trembling. "I love you nigga and you don't even know this bitch!" She cried. She mugged my face with her hand and shoved it, then turned and left.

"Tiff!" I yelled to her back but she kept going until she was out the door. Both of my mommas gave me evil glares. "Fuck!" I yelled and punched a hole in the wall.

————⋙◉⋘————

Just as Cool's funeral, Oil Can's was just as uncomfortable. I went up to see my brother for the last time. So many memories flooded my mind. The time I let him whoop my ass cause I had whooped his. And the time momma tore both of our asses up. The way he swore he was fly in Jr.high with a bunch of gold. His first car.

Now he was gone. Jaden and Tiffany were on their best behavior. Malicia handled herself well and comforted everybody with her smile. She looked at me crazy a few times and I knew that Tiffany had told her what happened. Tiffany and I hadn't talked since. She refused too.

After all the rituals of the funeral I went home to see the camera men and reporters' point of view of my brother. The headline read; *Gang Leader Mourned.*

"Today, city officals of Pine Bluff provided needed security for the farewell of Javon Allen. Cofounder of a streetgang that goes by The Moniker of Trapstah. Allen was murdered last Saturday, after being released from jail only fourty eight hours prior, and that was after making bond *on* a murder charge. Gangleaders and members came and went to pay their respects without a fuss or a tussle." The reporter stated and then there was a shot of me and Tiffany getting out the limo.

"Look at that shit." I said to Jaden who was laying beside me in the bed. "Shit still don't seem real."

"Fa real." Jaden said and gave my thigh a gentle squeeze. "Man. Baby I got yo back, not like your brother cause can't nobody replace him, but I got yo back!" Jaden said and I needed that. "Thanks baby." I told her eyes. And it seemed as if something in them. I just it took as if I was tripping. And I was, cause I had went and murdered a mothafucka everyday from the night Oil Can died until he was in the ground.

Dope Money by Yo Gotti kicked in and I grabbed the business phone off my night stand. "What it is?" I asked?

"Ya'll ready?" The connect answered with a question.

"Already." I said rubbing Jaden's thigh.

"Bet." The connect confirmed fifty more and hung up. "Ay, you still want to be my Almond Joy on South Beach?" I asked placing the phone back.

"Already boo!" Jaden pecked my lips. "That's what's up!" She said all girly. And then blessed me with some of the best head this side of the Mississippi.

Two days later Malicia and momma came by and picked me up.

"What you girls up to?" I asked getting in the back behind Malicia.

"Nothin! Bout to go shopping!" Malicia said.

"I just got to have these new Jordans!" Momma said getting into traffic.

"Tell me about it!" Malicia cosigned.

"Fa real!" I affirmed. I looked out my window. "Why you ain't been answering your phone?" I asked Malicia and patted the top of her head.

"Daddy!" She jumped and looked at momma. "Did he mess it

up?" She looked at me and smirked.

"Naah you aight!" Momma smiled and looked at me through the rear view. I dropped my head. "Daddy, and please don't shoot me off, but what's up with you and mom?"

"We tripping Me-Me." I kept it real with her. "You know I love her to death. I dunno!"

"Ya'll need to quit acting!" Malicia said. And I had went so far off in my thoughts that when I finally looked up we were pulling in Tiffany's driveway.

"I thought we were going shopping?" I asked neither in particular.

"No, were going shopping!" Momma pointed at Me-Me then herself. "You're going to talk to Tiff!" I got out and was about to knock when Tiffany opened it and let me in.

"What's up?' I asked. She smelled like she was fresh out of the tub. "Shit. What's up?" Tiffany said walking back up her hall with her nice booty sashaying to and fro in her short shorts. I caught up and took her arm.

"Jaden!" I said the wrong name and she turned around and slappped the shit out of me and started crying. I had to fix this. "Let me finish!" I grabbed her and she tried to get loose but to no avail. "Jaden and I are through!"

"Fuck you!" She yelled then spat in my face. I felt it run down my face. I had to gain control. I shoved her against the wall. "I love you nigga!" I said with my screwface and put my fist to her temple. "Remember that shit!" I bumped my fist against her head.

"Do you love her?" Tiffany cried watching my eyes.

"Did you hear what the fuck I just said!" I said close enough to her face that my lips touched her forehead.

"Then let her go! Let her go Octavious!" Tiffany said looking up at me with her pretty eyes. Flashes of good times ran through my mind. The way we talked all night. The way we made love. The next thing I knew I was kissing her neck.

"No! No OG!" Tiffany wailed as my kisses turned her anger into passion. "Quit OG! Don't do me like this!" she gave little resistance as I moved to her mouth. We got so caught up that we had to stop to catch our breath. We just looked at each other. "Leave OG. Don't do me like this!" Tiffany said but it was too late. I was back on her neck then bit her titties through her tank top. "Nooo! Octavious!" Tiffany moaned as she rubbed my head. I lifted the top and stuck my tongue in her belly button. She sucked in air through her teeth. This was her spot. "OG! Stop!" She moaned all sexy and I threw one leg over my shoulder and started sucking on her clitoris. "God! Oooh God! Octavious!" Tiffany screamed and her juices came flowing. I placed some hickies on the inside of a thigh, then threw the other one over my other shoulder and ate her pussy giving her two more nutts. I picked up her and took my dick out and eased her down on it andfucked her hard in the middle of the hall. "OG! It feels so good!" Tiffany yelled passionately.

"You like that dick?" I asked with a screwface and slammed her down on my dick.

"I love your dick!" Tiffany screamed and we caught a rythm.

"Who's juice box is this?" I asked and started showing out.

"This your juice box! Aah! Ah shit! I'm cumming! Mothafucka!" Tiffany yelled and came. I felt mine coming and exploded inside her so strong that my knees gave and I fell backwards. Tiffany landed on top of me and glowed big time and giggled.

We ended up fucking in the shower, in the kitchen, in Me-Me room, and then the front room. "I'm ready baby!" Tiffany said while stretched out on top of me. "I know you can't just ditch her, so you got two weeks OG. I'm not playing with yo ass neither!"

"I miss you so much Tiff. Since the first day I got out I been wanting your companionship. But you know it was all on you." I said and pecked her lips. "So you ready huh?"

"Yes, I love you Octavious!" Tiffany smiled and glowed. "So all the hoes you been fucking, that's over with!"

"Damn!"

"What?" Tiffany screwfaced.

"Already!" I said and palmed her ass.

Pimp was now second in command and my right hand man, and was handling his businesss. We were still at war with two clicks and was still holding it down. I finally got a chance to escape a week after the Tiffany episode and took Jaden to Miami. We decided to do a phot shoot while we were here. We drove our rented Tahoe straight to our hotel and had lunch. "This place is beautiful! All these different nationalities and people of colors!" Jaden said eating a fruit salad.

"Fa real!" I agreed. Miami was a sexy city and I had seen about a hundred women I wanted to fuck at the moment. Then for the thousandth time I thought about Tiff. I had a week left to kick it with Jaden. How would I tell her the business?

"OG! Boy you been doing that shit all week!" Jaden expressed with concerned eyes. She was just too beautiful to be so gangsta. "You want to talk about it?"

"Nawl it ain't nothing. Missing Oil Can." I meant but not at the time. I felt uneasy about telling her that I was calling it quits, at the same though I wanted her to run Trapstah Ladies, since her co-leader was still missing.

It was a beautiful hot day as we strolled in Miami traffic. the vehicles ranged from Donks to Ferraris to Maybachs. A Donk on twenty sixes strolled beside us sitting as high as the Tahoe we were in. South Beach was alive and jumping with booty, booty, booty, rocking everywhere. "Nigga you in pussy heaven ain't you?" Jaden smiled at me.

"That applies for you too, yo ass ain't slick!" I said and she blushed. "N-E-Way!"

"N-E-Way my ass! I betcha I get more numbers than you!" I challenged.

"Bet nigga!" Jaden accepted and we locked pinky fingers.

We got out and walked the beach for a while. Jaden was looking like eye candy in a Gucci two piece. She was carrying the matching sandals. Her diamonds were flawless. I took some good photos of her booty as it sashayed left to right. She had that little gap between her thighs that made her mouth watering. I now hated for it to end but I had to follow my heart and that was with Tiff. Bacause I know through thick or thin, she's going to love a nigga regaurdless. I got some good shots of Jaden in the water and on the sand. She was a natural for the camera. Two snowbunnies walked by with tans and asses like sistahs.

"Ay, may I ask one of ya'll a question?" I said to both.

"Shoot!" The shorter one aked. "Do ya'll think she's beautiful?" I asked while snapping shots and Jaden continued to pose.

"She's hot!" The other one with blond hair complemented.

"Yeah she's sexy!" That was shorty.

"Well, I'm OG and that's Jaden and she thinks that you two are the sexiest women on the beach, and wants ya'll to join her photo shoot!" "Well, okay!" Shorty said.

"I'm Misty and this is Teresa! My girlfriend!" Misty said and pecked Teresa on the lips. Teresa blushed.

"Already!" Jaden and I said in unison.

—⸻◆⸻—

Misty and Teresa turned out to be some real freaks. They had joined Jaden's shoot and she got them so heated that we had to go back to the room. We watched them get down, then fucked ourselves.

"Them hoes was wild!" Jaden said fresh out of the shower. "You see Misty's clit! Like a damn dick!" She sat on the edge of the bed and fired up a blunt.

"Fa real!" I agreed tired from busting two good nuts with Jaden. It seemed as if now was a good time to tell Jaden the business cause I was really tired of holding it from her. "Jaden, baby I got something to tell you and it is what it is." I said looking in her eyes.

"Shoot." Jaden said with a small hint of concern.

"It's about Tiff. We decided to get back together. And I can't help it Jaden. I love her. *We* love each other and it's nothing to do with you. I want you around Jaden, you're perfect for Trapstah Ladies and please stick with me on this, please understand." I said with pleading eyes.

"I understand." Jaden said and patted my leg and handed me the blunt. She got up and turned her back to me. "I got something to tell you too." She said and I figured it to be about her child. "I've been on a mission since we met. Actually me *and* Lamira." Jaden said and turned around and had a gun with a silencer.

"What the...?" I asked in shock.

"Yeah nigga, I'm workin. ESP! Know them?"

"Fuck you bitch!" I said with a screwface.

"You done that! And you're good! N-E-Way, Lamira's stupid ass got all in her feelings and got pregnant. Then she got ole boy killed at that party. So when she came up missing I knew what was up. So I had to buy myself some time and I did. Right before Oil Can got out I brought a phone indentical to Lamira's and put it in his bathroom. I knew he would check it and he called the exact number I wanted him to. I acted as the kidnapper, *and* as a screaming Lamira and got a hundred thou!" Jaden said and smiled at me. I thought about going for my gun but she read my mind. "Looking for this?" Jaden asked and opened her robe. She was fully dressed with my gun in her waist.

"N-E-Way, like I said, I had to buy some time. So when Oil came to give me my money, I had to leave with his Trapstah chain, which gave me more time with ESP to get the connect. And thanks to you, you gave it to me the night after the funeral, when the connect called and gave you more work. When you went to sleep I called back and let's just say, we talked a little business." Jaden finished and pointed her gun at me.

"You killed my brotha?" I asked with anger etched into my face. "Bitch you killed my mothafuckin brah?"

"By OG!" Jaden smiled. "It's been nice knowing you!" She blew a kiss and I tried to rush her and she shot me in the shoulder. "You know Tiffany's next. I might spare Me-Me for the sake of *my* daughter. "Jaden said and shot me again in the stomach.I fell back on the bed. I didn't want to die like this.

"Ay, you know what?" I asked with a smile and tasted blood in my mouth.

"Shoot! Before I shoot!" Jaden smirked at her own joke and turned her head to the side. She put another silent bullet in my thigh.

"Fuck!... I hope I see you in the after life, I'mma fuck you up you punk ass bitch!" I said and prepared myself for my exit into the next life. Malicia's face popped in my mind. Her smile and her joyous ways. I'll never get to see her graduate or go on to college. I closed my eyes. It was over with.

"Nooo!" Another voice said and I opened my eyes to see a butcher knife sidways in Jaden's neck with the look of panic in her face. She dropped the gun and grabbed her neck and tried to pull the knife out. She fell to her knees, and standing there was my savior that I knew all to well.

Chapter 24
"Tiffany"

I just knew something was wrong. I could feel it. Jaden had always been suspicious to me. Especially after the night Oil Can got killed when she had supossedly been woke up out her sleep but yet she had on make up. And then her hair was flawless and not wrapped up. And I could have swore I smelled perfume when I got in her face that night. The same scent that was at that apartment Oil got killed in. I was sitting at home alone about to play with myself fantasizing about OG's ass when my phone rung. "Hey baby!" I said like a teenager in love. "South Beach? What?" I was instantly mad enough to shoot a pistol. "What are you doing OG?"

"We just going to do a shoot. I promised it a while back and you already know I don't break promises." OG said. "That's what's up." I saluted his pride even though I didn't want him to go. "I love you boo!"

"I love you too shawty!" OG said and I blushed. I loved it when he called me that. OG hung up but something was still hanging in the air.

Jaden. I did not trust that bitch and then I really went thinking crazy like maybe, just maybe, her and OG was planning to run off together. And that wouldn't leave me for shit.

———◦((◦))◦———

Since I didn't have shit else to do, I talked Me-Me and momma off to Magic Springs and caught the same flight as OG and Jaden. I should've been majoring in stalking a nigga cause I was good at it. I played the back ground through the photo shoot and some little episode with some white girls. The white girls left then I seen something. Jaden came out the hotel and got into a Chrysler 300 with Arkansas tags. And for some odd reason I got scared. Jaden got out and went back into the hotel. I followed her back in and watched her to their room. I walked back and forth in front of their door trying to listen. I had even changed my walk just in case they opened the door and saw me out here. I had also went and bought a knife from Wal-Mart cause to tell the truth, I was scared of Jaden. Then all of a sudden I heard some cursing. Then a soft sound. Then I heard OG yell *fuck you bitch!*' I ran down to the front desk and talked the clerk out of another key, with a thirty dollar tip of course, and eased myself into their room. I thought I was tripping when I made it to the bedroom of their suite. Jaden's back was to me but OG was bleeding from his leg, stomach, and shoulder. His eyes was closed. Jaden pointed something and I was up on her before I knew it and stuck the knife in her neck. I ran to OG.

"Baby!" I cried cradling his head as I dialed 911 on my phone and told them the situation.

"Tiff." OG said and his breath reeked of blood. I seen consciousness leaving his eyes. "Tell Me-Me to graduate and go to college for me."

"OG don't!" I cried. You better not leave me! Baby don't leave me! I can't live without you!" I was now holding him tight with his blood soaking up in my clothes. His head was dangling like a baby.

"Tiff. I...Love you shawty, you be good." OG strained out and I heard the police in the background. I prayed over and over that they came in time to save his life, my love, my OG.

———⟨⟨◉⟩⟩———

The police came and an ambulance took OG to the hospital. I was allowed to ride in the ambulance and it seemed like we couldn't go fast enough. OG was in bad shape and if he made it, he would go directly to Intensive Care. I called Ms.Ann. Her and MeMe were on the first thing smoking this way. Even though I had saved OG's life and pleaded self defense, I had to go turn myself in on a man-slaugter charge. Three days later Pimp and a bail bondsman came and got me and we headed back to the hospital.

"Hey shawty!" OG said from his bed. He was out of Intensive Care and Malicia was at his side playing with his fingers.

"He mad at me momma. I ate all his Jello!" Malicia said and opened her arms at me for a hug. "I missed you momma!"

"I missed you too baby!" I said as Ms.Ann kissed my forehead.

"Thank you so much Tiff for saving my baby!" Ms.Ann passionately said and we hugged faces. A tear fell from her eye and onto my cheek. "I love you!"

"I love you too momma!" I kissed her forehead.

"Baby, you scared me. I was praying so hard!" I said rubbing OG's eyebrows.

"Thanks, girl, you saved a nigga life. I owe you one." OG said and grabbed my fingers. "You know what I want!" I siad blushing at what I wanted.

"Oh Lord! Momma!" Malicia said embarrassed at my thoughts. Me and that girl was too close. "Come on momma let's leave these love birds alone!" She said to Ms.Ann and they left. "Fa real though, you know what I want!" I waved my ring finger at him.

"Already shawty! Already!"

———⇒«(◊)»⇐———

Two months later that finger had one of the biggest rocks that Sissy's Log Cabin could give me. "Guess what time it is?" OG said to me. We had Malicia stretched out on the floor.

"It's Tickle Time!" I cheered and OG tickled her ass to death! She loved it so much that she tired us out! We now had a house way out in Watson Chapel and since then my love life has been out of this world. It's been too good cause I was a month pregnant. The only thing I hated was that OG and his click was still at war with some other gang. He would recieve calls in the middle of the night and would be gone. Pimp was now around as if he was Oil Can's replacement and he was nice and respectful.

"Baby, can you run and get MeMe some allergy medicine?" I asked. Her sinuses were brothering her or she'd done caught a summer cold.

"Aight. You need something?" OG asked grabbing his keys and I caught him staring at my ass. "That's why my ass pregnant now! Nawl I'm straight!" I said and he pecked my neck. Gone boy! Before you start something!" As soon as his ass left I was missing him. The doorbell rung and I just knew it was him playing like he always do. I opened the door and a pimple face white boy with ballons was standing there.

"Hello Tiffany Green! These are for you!" Pimple Man smiled.

"Awe, that's sweet!" I smiled and balloon man moved and a tall handsome guy was standing there.

"They're from me!" Handsome man said.

"Who are you!" I asked wondering why.

"I'm Popcorn!"